THE WIDOW'S WILL

BOOK III: NURSING HER WRATH SERIES

EMELLE ADAMS

DEDICATION

For Tony, whose combination of patience and exuberance helps me no end. You are amazing.

In memory of Jack 'the hat' Drever, who would kindly check my punctuation. I miss getting told off for my comma habit.

Thanks to Adam, Mum, Dave, John, Tara, and Maria for listening, reading first drafts and going on road trips to potential murder sites around East Lothian.

PROLOGUE

I NEVER REALISED DIGGING a grave would be so difficult. On television, they produce a perfect rectangular hole in minutes, with a neat pile of dirt next to it, ready for filling in—after they've checked for car headlights, passers-by and dog walkers, that is. I didn't reckon on this! Roots, stones and random things in the way! An old brick. A broken milk bottle. Things that make no sense in a field, unless someone else hid something around here ... another body maybe...

ONE

RHIANNON

'*I CONVERSED with a punk from Loanhead on the Innocent Railway Path as he collected hemlock to fashion into jewellery,*' I scribble in my fresh notebook. No sentence one considers writing can ever be entirely original, but surely that hadn't been written down before. What resonates with me about this short interaction is how I'm not taken aback by this type of occurrence. Nothing shocks me to my core these days. Plus, to my benefit, I now know where to harvest hemlock if required.

I had risen early for one of my striding-out walks. It was one of those rare warm, sunny Scottish mornings that did not require a coat. Early on a Saturday is the best time for marching and thinking, I believe. The Friday night party people were still in bed, and with no morning commuters, it was remarkably quiet in the town, apart from the seagulls. On my return leg to the flats, my peace was disrupted by music. At first, its source or genre was undiscernible, until, coming closer and closer, I eventually recognised it—'I Want to Break Free' by Queen. Yards in front of me, Preston's bright orange car spun into the flats' car park, windows open. He was early. By the time I caught up with him, he was already retrieving a cardboard box from his hatchback.

'Cannae believe I'm here again,' he mumbled in place of hello, scanning the flats from top to bottom. Grabbing a couple of bags from the boot, I led the way.

'In you come.' I gestured once we reached the main door. It had been fixed at last, so I waved the tag and it clicked open. He hesitated, announcing, 'Oh well! Time to swallow the bullet.' Then he proceeded into the communal hallway.

I opened my mouth to quiz him about what he meant but reconsidered and shut it again with a shake of my head. More of Preston's unusual phrases and malapropisms were to be expected in the weeks to come, so I'd better get used to it. We progressed up the sole flight of stairs to my flat.

'Home sweet house,' muttered Preston, as I granted him access to the flat itself. I handed over his personal key from the dresser, placing it atop the box he was balancing.

'I'm in the second bedroom now?' he said, less a question than a statement. Nudging open the door with his foot, he strode in and set the box on the bed.

'Aye,' I answered, following him in.

'You've taken my old room, I notice.' Preston carried on, 'I must remember not to barge in on you in the middle of the night!'

'I imagine I'll be safe enough,' I retorted, dumping his bags.

'Well, dinnae be sleepwalking into my space when you're feeling lonely, or I'll have to prop a chair up against the door.'

'Sleep with one with eye open,' I mock warned him, wagging my finger.

'And don't you be murdering me in my sleep...' He trailed off, running his fingers through his hair. I contemplated the floor, sensing the heat rising up my neck.

'And you are fine with the dog and the cat?' Preston sang, tilting his head to the side.

'They should be fine. My cats are placid things. When do you get them back?'

'Well, Uncle Geoff and Auntie Jerry looked after Willie and Boabie while I was in the you-know-where.' He paused.

'Prison! You can say it!' I blurted out, hoping he wouldn't take offence. As he often dishes out smart comments, I felt assured he wouldn't. For now, however, he remained silent.

'I know where you've been residing,' I added—tentatively, due to his lack of response. Sensing his discomfort, I returned to the safe subject of the animals. 'Are they not attached to the pets now?'

'Yeah, but they're too old to be bothered long-term. So, Tuesday.' He stared, lips pursed, towards the living room. I followed his path of vision.

'Come on, it's fine.' I reassured him, leading him along the corridor. Preston entered the living room with baby steps and perched on the edge of the sofa, facing the scene of the crime.

'I wondered if I'd be all right coming back here,' he whispered, as if the dead could hear.

'After the fire?' I circled around the obvious this time, hoping Preston would open up about the killing himself.

'No, not the fire! The murder! Full fine you know! Are you training to be a counsellor or something? Cannae ask a straight question. Believe me, I've had my fill of that crowd—counsellors and do-gooders. "How do you feel, Mr. Field? What do *you* think, Mr. Field?" Well, I said to them, "I'm paying you. You tell me!" Money for nothing, that malarkey. I could be a counsellor myself by now— that's if they'd employ a convict. I attended a few courses inside about "listening". That's what they called it. I'm no built for listening, let me tell you.' He giggles, then in a second, he looks sombre, his eyes fix on the corner of the room where his brother drew his last breath.

'Oh, your poor brother.'

'That bastard! No, don't feel sorry for him having his throat slit. He had it coming, believe you me. It's the vision of him bleeding all over the furniture and the carpet. You should have seen the mess.' He shuddered, drawing his gaze along the skirting, as if looking for evidence.

'There's not a mark. I checked.'

'Did you?' He screwed up his face. Turning to me, he smiled a tight-lipped smile.

I nodded, grappling for something to say. 'And no ghosts.' I butted in on the silence.

'Good, he haunted me when he was alive. He's in a better place now—the pit of hell.' He shook himself out of his reflection by jumping up, clapping his hands, and announcing, 'I'd better get organised. I've another run, at least. And we've a long day tomorrow. I hate bloody funerals. I'm bringing Jan for extra moral support, by the way.'

'Oh! Have you heard from her?' I asked, as we ambled along the corridor to the front door.

'Oh, aye. She even wrote to me in prison,' he replied, not missing a step.

A gasp escaped my mouth, hopefully not heard by Preston. *What the hell did she have to write to him about?*

He halted, twisting on the handle. 'Kept me well informed,' he whispered, with a knowing nod, before shutting the door behind him and leaving me dazed in the hall.

Shit!

TWO

LYSSA

'AT LAST,' I announce aloud, as I smooth down my black dress and view myself in the mirror. I sigh. I suit black, I decide, despite those who say that pastels go better with my white-blonde hair. Duncan arranged for my colours to be "done" by a woman in Royal Crescent, in Edinburgh. She said black wasn't technically one of my colours, as it should drain me, but I look super slim at least. I'll pop on a red lip.

Yes, I look good. Good to go. And I must go. She is—*was*—my only sister. I can't get out of it. Angela's funeral takes place today. Now and then, events like these have to be suffered. I'm sure they will say I carried out my duties with grace and dignity, and I suppose that is the best I can hope for.

I knew it was coming. She has been ill for a long time. In a big way, it is a relief. There is one single thing worse than being shot, and that is waiting to be shot, Duncan always says. It puts a final score through this whole sorry mess, this nightmare, but this final hurdle needs to be jumped over before that finishing line.

When Angela was convicted for murder and sent to prison, she named me as her next of kin, despite having a son. She didn't want Callum bothered at university. I agreed, although I wasn't happy about it. Duncan said it was my duty, he supposed. It meant dealing with the prison liaison officer while she was in there. I discovered that when inmates are taken to prison, they make a list of contacts, including who to contact if the inmate dies in custody. She chose me.

If she had died in prison, it would have been a lot more convenient. They might have arranged the whole thing, a burial or cremation at the prison. Her body would have remained in their hospital, in custody. Over time, she deteriorated, so they ruled she would pose no danger to the public. They released her on compassionate grounds to die in a hospice. In short, the prison washed their hands of her, shoved her out to a ward. Then she became my problem.

The hassle of that burden was almost too much to bear; that, and the bloody embarrassment of trying to keep my head down in the village, rather than answer questions about my murdering sister. I took to walking the doggos at five in the morning, in case I met anyone. The golf and tennis club socials were the worst. As Duncan Whatmore's wife, I was forced to show face. I have some status about me. People know who I am.

At least, being married, I have a different surname from Angela. Outwith this area, many people never made the connection. Another positive is that we live up the hill, in Inveresk Village, with the mansion houses and footballing neighbours and politicians. The million-pound houses are set away from the town gossips. It's comforting to be sandwiched between the seaside town and the mining villages further inland, but somehow separate, exclusive.

Duncan isn't here, of course. That's the worst part of having a husband who works away; I have to do so much on my own. There are benefits to that, too, I must admit. The girls at the club say they're jealous, as at least he isn't under my feet all day. The house becomes untidier during his stays, it's true, but I still hate it when he leaves. However, it's the price I pay for the lifestyle we lead. He has to work to pay for everything, so he travels for months at a time. There's a lot of money to be made for a bomb disposal expert in the Middle East.

He always makes up for it when he comes home. Then, by the end of his stint here, I'm almost ready for the rest. I miss him today, however.

IT'S WALKING distance from our home to the church and burial ground. For luck, I touch the antique crucifix on the wall on the way out, say goodbye to my wee doggos, and close the door. I barely have to turn the corner outside the gates to see the graveyard. All our family is buried here. I hate cemeteries.

Walking in the crisp air, I teeter on the uneven ground under my high heels. I might go over on my ankle and miss Pilates for weeks.

I hope there isn't a big turnout. Angela's death at such a youngish age is tragic, but slitting a man's throat did not endear her to anyone. She acted psychotic, caused by the brain tumour for sure, but nevertheless ... she went far too far.

She always did.

THREE

RHIANNON

PRESTON, standing stock-still, peers up at the ceiling in the hall, as if it might become translucent if he concentrates hard enough.

'Who's in Angela's flat? Her lad, Callum? I heard footsteps.' Without waiting for an answer, he straightens his black tie and holds the door open for me to exit to the waiting taxi.

'He's there now and then,' I answer, although Preston may have been asking rhetorical questions. 'He never came back much after his mum's trial. Lived with his dad for a while.'

'Mmm, he might have come back last night, for the funeral. We'll see him today, I suppose,' he whispers, so Callum won't hear.

'Yeah.' I nod.

Preston's volume increases once we settle into our seats in the black cab. 'I know Angela was ill, but I grew used to her fighting on. I forgot she'd go. It's an end to the whole thing, I suppose. A full stop.' He takes an audible breath. 'Lyssa will be there—her sister.'

Feeling tense, I nod again. Preston continues, 'Oh yeah. I forgot you knew—'

'—I attended school with them both,' I manage to utter in a failed attempt to shut him up.

'I met Lyssa a couple of times through Ange. She'll be there with her man maybe. She never came near much. They're loaded; lives up the hill in Inveresk, the stuck-up cow.' He states this in a matter-of-fact, almost pitying manner, rather than with any venom.

'Really?' Of course, I am aware of that already, but I prefer his talking to awkward silence. Preston leaving spaces in any conversation unnerves me.

'Yeah, he's minted. She never worked a day in her life. A bit of beauty stuff, then landed on her feet with the rich old man, or so said Angie baby.' He swallows his last words with a gulp.

'Callum will inherit the flat,' I surmise at random.

'Yeah, but I doubt he'll want to live there. Too many memories.'

We let up with the conversation, running out of things to say. I stare out of the window at those in the sunshine, all carrying on with their lives, unaware of death. Only we are confronted with *that* reality today.

'Where are you going to work now, Preston?' I venture after a minute. 'Now that you're ... you're ... out.' I speak in code to spare the eavesdropping taxi driver.

'I've a few options.' He ponders for second. 'There is the old village pub. I might re-join that workforce and resurrect my career in comedy.'

I contort my face. 'Where Kim threw Darren down the cellar?' I blurt out my theory, wondering whether Preston will be shocked.

He takes it in his stride. 'Maybe he fell. We'll never know now, with Kim gone too.' Preston's eyes dart towards me.

A surge of anxiety travels through my body, causing me to flinch. I hope he deduces my reaction is due to my dislike of Kim, not because I murdered her. My relationship with Kim's husband, Rob, could have crossed his mind. Perhaps he'll assume the whole episode is still a sore subject. It is. The guilt, and the lost love.

'They always want staff at the old folks' home,' he continues.

'God! You'd see Mum.' I groan, and then add, 'And Rob's mum.' It dawns on me that this is the first time I've voiced his name out loud since he was imprisoned for Kim's murder. It sticks in my throat, and I struggle to swallow.

'Hell, that's a point. Imagine those two mums together. Have they not killed each other yet?'

I leave Preston's question hanging and return to staring out the window. That's plenty of talk of murders around here for one day.

'Or I could try the pub in the High Street,' Preston babbles on. 'I'm sure my criminal record will go against me. Although I could say folk might want to come in and see the murderer as an attraction —I mean, the guy who tried to hide the body with Angela,' he corrects himself.

I catch the driver glancing at Preston in his rear-view mirror.

'But I suppose I opened that can of worms, so now I'll need to lie in it.' Preston seems flustered.

The taxi comes to a halt.

'Here we are. There's a good turnout,' I say, because that is what people always say.

FOUR

LYSSA

I CAN'T BELIEVE Debbie showed up. I spot her backside waddling ahead of me. Her arse is wider than the Clyde these days. *She'll need to watch her calories, or she won't be able to fit into her tennis skirt.* That reminds me, with her as a witness, I'll be the talk of the tennis club once more. Debbie needn't get on her moral high horse, though. Her greasy spoon café is closed again by environmental health. I'd never set foot in there. I rarely spend time in the town. I prefer heading right up Edinburgh, somewhere decent.

Who's that she is chatting to? Julie, my cleaner. I can't imagine they'd get on. But maybe Julie cleans for her, too. Debbie should get her into the café to give it the once or twice over. Or run around it herself for a bit of exercise and lay off the bacon butties.

I catch a glimpse of Callum. I nod, and he nods back. He's a nice boy. Things will be better for him now that his mum is gone. He needs to get on with his life and finish his masters. He is better off living with his dad, although he has a girlfriend now, from Glasgow, so I suppose that will be the next thing.

Jen and Jill, who worked with Angela, are here, too, I see. I can't imagine wanting to associate with a killer if you didn't have to. Of course, now they're witnesses to my presence as well. Bloody rubberneckers are lined all the way up to the church door. I notice a camera crew lurking outside the gates. My sister became somewhat of a celebrity when her ramblings were published by that pal of hers, Tara. And there is madam herself, swanning around, grinning for the cameras. Honestly, have they nothing better in their diaries? I'm so glad I decided to wear a wide-brimmed disc hat. One tip of my head and my face is obscured. I copied Kate Middleton there.

INSIDE THE CHURCH, I take my place in the front row. Angela and I were both baptised here and used to attend Sunday school in this church, before mother's dramatic Billy Graham-type conversion. I attend kirk every Sunday. I've come a long way from the terraced houses down the hill, where I shared a bunk bed with an apparent psychopath. No, I mustn't say that about her. The brain tumour affected her thinking. Angela was never positive, though. Overweight, negative, always complaining—she never sorted her life out, so I believe she brought it on by herself. Her self-pity was pitiful. One has only to think positive and good things will come. I knew I'd live well, because I always believed I deserved it.

People like Angela are negative thinkers. It comes out in their words and their actions, and they wonder why their lives are rubbish. It also applies to their bodies. They put crap in, therefore they look crap on the outside. I told her many times, but she never listened. I'm all for positive vibrations, manifesting your own positive life. And here I am, with Duncan, living in my fabulous house, living my best life. I'm proof. I feel myself smiling, but I put a lid on that. I'm in church, after all.

As I settle into my seat, I catch Preston's eye. I purse my lips at the thought of a jailbird just parked there like butter wouldn't melt. Angela's partner in crime. Look at him, sitting with John, Susan and Paul, Rhiannon, and some great big fat woman I don't recognise.

Mind you, all fat people look the same to me. Tara is now joining that lot. Tara should know better. She is a different class, at least—Lady Tara—but too loud, too out there in my opinion. She's into all sorts of hippy nonsense and is always making a show of herself. *Why is she mingling with that rubbish?*

If it wasn't for Preston, Angela would never have killed Preston's bother. He was in Preston's flat at the time, after all. She made out Preston's brother abused her as a child, but I have no recollection of that. She mentioned this abuse to me once, and I told her so. It was all attention-seeking rubbish, I told her. Nothing happened to me at our holidays at the caravan at North Berwick, and I was the bonny one.

It's all *me too* these days. But it is more like *me, me, me,* if you ask me. I mean why bring it up all those years later, even if it did happen? She should have said so at the time! But no, years later she regurgitates it all, wanting someone else to blame for her drinking, her unhealthy attitude to food, her bad decisions.

I hear the minister say. 'Let us pray.'

I bow my head in respect for the dead.

FIVE

LYSSA

I FEEL my face screwing up as I enter the stairway and head up the stairs. Callum asked folks back to Angela's flat after the funeral. I tried to get out of it by saying I had to walk my doggos, but he insisted, so I've bitten my lip and dragged myself there, making sure I arrive last. I'll use my fur babies as an excuse to sneak away early.

I hold my breath as I step up to landing number one, knowing what went on there: a bloodbath. I stall, as the vision of my own sister dragging a body downstairs to the bins flutters through my mind. I shudder.

'Hiya!'

I shriek, as Preston pops his head around the door. *Good god. Why is he in there? Has he returned to the scene of the crime? They say they do that.*

I take a step back.

'I've some sloe gin, Angela's favourite,' he announces, slamming the door behind him, leaving me frozen to the spot. He bounds up the stairs in front of me. Static with confusion, I fixate on the door. Surely, he doesn't live here now? I know he used to. I know he hid the body from here. I cringe again. I'll never understand it.

Shaking myself out of my stupor, I face the last set of stairs. Callum's bound to get the flat in the will. The sooner he sells it, the better, and we can get on with our lives. I force myself to plod upwards to another socially awkward situation.

'Alyssa,' says Rhiannon.

We went to school together, but you'd never guess. She looks at least twenty years older than me.

'Yes,' I answer, although it wasn't a question. I scan her up and down. Not fat, at least, but her hair is a mess, and she wears not a scrap of makeup. She looks dirty. I curl my lip at the crumbs on her lapel, wondering why Rob would ever have left Kim for her, let alone the rest of that sordid story ...!

'I live downstairs.'

Her words snap me out of my judgement. 'Where? Downstairs from where?'

'Here. Downstairs from here, in the flat below.'

'Ah,' I say, but nothing more. The least said the better. But I see! It's Rhiannon's flat now, not Preston's anymore. I quickly work out that Preston and Rhiannon must be pals or even flatmates. I'm smart like that. I'm handed a sloe gin, which I will nurse. I'll not poison my body with that muck.

'Jan, this is Alyssa, Angela's sister,' Rhiannon says to the fat one.

'I prefer Lyssa these days.'

'Okay, Lyssa. Didn't you change your name to Monique in fifth year?'

She's had a few too many drinks already. I glower at her.

'Yeah, you did! You said it suited you better.' She laughs. So does the fat one, and I stare them out. I don't see anything funny.

'She lives in Inveresk Village,' Rhiannon slurs.

'Ooh, very posh,' her chubby pal adds.

I smile at the fat one but turn again to Rhiannon. 'How's Jocelyn doing?'

'Great—lives in Spain now.' She rambles on about her sister. I let her babble on.

'Can I speak to you, Preston?' Debbie calls from the back of the room.

'Aye, nae bother,' he answers. Debbie waddles over to him, and I overhear their tete-a-tete.

'You need some work?'

'Maybe,' he half sings.

'I'm short at the café. I could do with some help a few days a week, and I've some renovation work planned. Could you cast your eye over it?'

'Aye OK. That sounds all right. I'll give you a call.'

God almighty. I'm definitely not going to Debbie's café now. The idea of being served a scone by a convict fills me with horror. My attention flits back to Rhiannon, who is still talking.

'... and she rarely comes over because she just met someone new out there, and things are going pretty well ...'

God knows what Rhiannon is blabbering on about. I've worked out another thing in common between Rhiannon and Preston. She was involved with a murder, too, after her affair with Rob Ritchie. He ended up killing his wife, Kim, over it. Rob went to our golf club, and Kim seemed pleasant enough. He'd strangled her on the lagoons with her own John Lewis scarf! If that's the kind of guy, he is, Rhiannon was lucky to get away without being throttled herself. What he saw in her is the bigger mystery to me. She's a real Plain Jane, not worth murdering over.

I make my excuses to leave, dabbing my eye with a perfect white handkerchief, hoping I look as gracious as Meghan Markle at the Queen's funeral. None of these folk are the type of people I want to mix with, but I'll have a story to tell at the golf club. I am glad, however, that I'll never have to be in the company of any of them ever again.

SIX

LYSSA

I'M POTTERING about the house today after speaking to Duncan on the phone in Saudi. He was named executor of Angela's will. I refused that auspicious job. It is not for me, all that technical bother. He never mentioned what it contained before, as he never bothered checking until necessary. He called our lawyer, Greg, to sort it out.

Some light housework gains me a little exercise, ready for the help coming in. I rarely sit down and slob about. I take regular Pilates classes, but if I keep moving the rest of the time, it all adds up to a calorie deficit. I need to prep the house for 'Rough-as-guts' Julie to come in. She is a horror, but she is thorough with the cleaning. 'Rough-as-guts' works in a few houses around here, so I don't want her telling tales to any of the others about my house being a hovel. She is bitchy and gossipy about everyone else, so I know she'll look for something. I also know she sprays my expensive perfume on herself when she leaves. I smell it and see the liquid going down, but I don't begrudge her that. I doubt she'd take anything substantial. It's not like she could force her lumpiness into any of my clothes. Anyway, she is cheap compared to my friends' cleaners in Edinburgh. She hasn't increased her prices in ten years. I know folk who pay double.

Angela left everything to Callum, except the lodge in Kenmore and the campervan, both of which were left to me. Of course, the lodge was originally Mother's. I don't mind the Kenmore Lodge. I like Perthshire well enough, although I prefer abroad, with the sun on my back. But the campervan? What the hell will I do with it? Duncan laughed aloud when he told me about it. He is a five-star hotel man. Camping is not our style. Glamping perhaps—"for the gram", as the young people say—but I'm young at heart, too. It is not even a brand-new one. It's an ancient twenty-year-old banger. Although, I looked it up, and it seems they sell for a decent price. I'll leave it parked up somewhere down the hill in town, and then I'll flog it. I'm not bringing it into the village for everyone to see. I might take the proceeds and head to Dubai.

I tidy the living room a little and plump the cushions. I believe it is important to maintain your house as much as possible yourself. Of course, I don't carry out the maintenance! We have a handyman on tap, and a regular gardener, but I monitor them. Duncan calls a man in for anything he would call "manual labour".

I love my house. We bought it ten years ago. Before then, the Smiths had lived in it since the sixties. These houses don't change hands too often, so we feel blessed to live here. It shows respect for yourself, to live in a decent, clean, and ordered environment. If you live in a piggery, you must consider yourself a pig, right?

I pick up some magazines and spread them across the coffee table, like they do in the actual magazines. I don't read books, just fashion articles and lifestyle magazines. I call them "my books".

Angela apparently left a folder to Preston in the will. It probably contains all her writing and notes. He's welcome to the psychotic ramblings of a mad woman. That sounds harsh, but it's true. She had this fantasy—her story being made into a novel. The arrogance! Tara took a copy of it all, twisted it around, added an ending and a couple of cops, and published it with my sister's blessing. She couldn't profit from it herself, but Tara did. I never read it.

I wander into the hall, past the locked door to Duncan's office.

My husband has been away six weeks now, in Saudi. He's due back next week, thank goodness. It's so much better having him around. I like a strong man who takes care of everything, so I don't have to worry. 'My office is sacred,' he always says. I never go in there. Even Rough-as-guts Julie is not allowed in. He cleans it himself. He's so funny about it. 'It's where I run my empire,' he says. I let him have his space. Men need a man cave. 'Everything is under control!' he always insists. He says that I deserve the princess treatment, and I agree, of course!

Through the window by the door, I see a police car pass the gate. Back and forth, it goes. I'm intrigued, but I shake my head. No more drama is due to come my way.

SEVEN

RHIANNON

'ARE you sure you want to open another?' I ask Jan, intercepting her in the hallway as I exit the toilet. She freezes on the spot, contemplating the second bottle of sloe gin. Her lips tight, she considers my question for a matter of seconds, then she bursts back into life. 'Yeah,' she answers. 'We'll be fine!' She pushes past me into the living room, undoing the bottle stopper as she goes.

'Oh, it's like the gang is back together,' she gushes, topping up the half-full glasses on the coffee table in front of us. She plonks herself down next to Preston. 'Except for Kim. To Kim,' she toasts, raising her glass.

Rolling my eyes, I throw myself down in the single armchair. My fingers claw at the corduroy rows on the seat beneath my thighs.

'Fuck's sake, Jan,' scolds Preston, his eyes wide and his head tipped towards me.

'What?' Jan stares at me blankly.

How can she not sense the tension? I clench my jaw as Preston brings Jan's attention back to him.

'Talk about bringing the party down. You're talking about Kim— the woman who bloody set fire to this place with Rhiannon in it. The woman who burnt her whole family to death when she was a bairn. That Kim?'

I unclench my jaw and let go of the chair material. I force relaxation, but it's not coming.

'She was okay to us, though, in the pub. And you shouldn't speak ill of the dead,' she whimpers.

'The Kim that near beat her husband to a pulp for years, driving him to kill her, and ...'

'Oh God, aye. But what a way to go, eh? Nobody deserves that. What the heck was Rob thinking? He should have just left her.'

I breathe in, using my diaphragm as I've learnt online, and attempting to appear unconcerned. Preston digs Jan in the ribs and half points at me, as if I won't notice.

'Oh, sorry Rhiannon. I forgot you went out with Rob ...'

Preston nods solemn-faced, but Jan rambles on with her head tilted, '... like behind Kim's back.'

Preston sighs. 'Jan, can you put your boot in it any further?'

I shift in my seat, hoping for a change of subject.

'What? Oh God! Sorry, I'm digging a hole here,' Jan whispers.

Preston giggles. 'I shouldn't laugh ... but, Jan, you *are* the limit.'

'Sorry I brought it up, but she's dead now, so all I can say is: God rest her soul.' Jan rushes another toast to the tormenting tart and downs another drink.

'Jesus wept! She'll no' be in heaven, that bitch!' Preston blurts out.

Jan puts her head down, and I feel a smile spread across my face. I decide to put Jan out of her misery. 'Preston told me you wrote to him in prison.'

She brightens up, raises her head, and shakes off any worry. 'Oh yeah. He was away ages before I heard from him. Four weeks, I waited. They wouldn't give you paper, would they, Preston?'

'No. It was rationed. Some story about COVID-19 causing delays. Everything was quarantined, even paper.'

'And then ... all of a sudden ... a brown envelope popped through the letterbox!'

I feel my face heating again.

Preston reads my mind. 'Ahem, suddenly? It's not like your phone pinged, Jan,' he says, reaching over for the olives.

Jan is unfazed. 'He had a number. They don't use their name, just a number. I was so excited. Terry thought I was mental. I said to him, I'm not writing to my lover on death row. I know the person, and it's Preston. You ken him fine.'

'And you couldn't phone me for ages either,' Preston adds.

'You called as well?' I butt in, too quickly. *What have these two had to talk about?*

'Things move so slowly in prison. Although, I suppose they aren't going anywhere, so there is no hurry to get them sorted out. The government maintains they care about human rights, but the screws ...'

'Screws! Get you!' Preston interjects, between munches. 'That's them! The screws, they love the power trip.'

'What was it like?' I ask him.

'I slept in a bunk bed with another fella, on a two-inch mattress.'

'Preston's letters read like a Trip Advisor review,' Jan interrupts, getting up to retrieve some snacks from the kitchen.

He carries on, regardless. 'I was a martyr to my back, but I'd made my prison bed, so I needed to lie in it. Then they moved me to single room with an actual mattress, proper, and a wardrobe. I've never been so excited to see a piece of furniture, let me tell you. Then I was moved, for good behaviour, to the open prison.'

'That sounds better.'

'Yes and no. I had a phone of my own and was allowed to wander about a bit. It was like boarding school, if you can imagine that, but I ended up back on a new two-inch mattress, sharing a room and bunk beds again. I'd say, "I'm stuck between a rock and the deep blue sea here."'

'And your sex life?' I smirk.

'It's not like on the telly. None. Nada. Nil.'

Jan returns. 'Me neither. Terry's away working loads, so he's always tired.'

Preston spins in his seat to face her. 'Random, Jan! But do continue ...'

'So, when he was away, I arranged a delivery. I bought a vibrator for the first time in my life!'

'What?' I snort my drink through my nose.

'No!' adds Preston, although he perches further forward on his chair.

'Yes! It says it's a body massager on the box, but it's not.'

'TMI.' Preston wrinkles his nose.

'And ...?' I question, alcohol getting the better of me

'And ... I don't want to know!' Preston lies.

'Disaster!' She answers

'OK, now I definitely want to know.'

'I sneaked it up the stairs and hid it. The bairn and I watched a film, and I thought I'd try it out later. Then, when I was in my bed, I read the instructions. It said it had four levels of power and there was another button that changed the pattern. Then, of course, I noticed it need charging up for three hours before use. This was at midnight, and I thought, *Not tonight, Josephine.*'

'Pfft!' Preston laughs towards me.

'Later, I woke up and checked the clock—3 am. Mind you, it came advertised as silent? Silent my arse! It came on at number four power in the dead of the night. A jet fighter taking off would have been quieter. I was flapping around in the dark, trying to turn it off, changing the rhythm to different settings. Eventually, it stopped. Then the bairn came in, saying, "I got woken up. I think someone is drilling next door." FYI, I'm a dab hand at the controls now.'

Preston jumps up. 'Shite! Would you look at the time? I need my bed. I've my first day at Debbie's café tomorrow. I cannae sit here with you two, burning the midnight oil from both ends.'

EIGHT

LYSSA

IN THE HALL, I damp dust the console table and top up the reed diffuser. Duncan will return soon, so I put the photos of his family back on the coach cabinet. (I store them in the drawer when he's not home; I've no need to see them.) I discover some room spray from Marks and Spencer and waft it around. I carry the flowers and vase back to the kitchen. I have a new bouquet on the counter to replace them, as these are getting tired. I arrange them on the kitchen bunker to place back on the console table later.

Duncan has little contact with his family. I call them his ex-family. They are all grown up now, in their thirties, so there's no need for them to bother their dad. The eldest somctimes comes by. Duncan says that when Jack and Carol show face, they're usually after money. Plain names suit them. His ex-wife, Stella, is drab and frumpy, too. I can't imagine what he saw in her. It's not fair, of course. I am younger, but not by much. People take me for half my age. She let herself go, I suppose. I'm in beauty, so I'm aware surgical enhancement can help, but self-maintenance is the key. I've had everything done possible, but I take care of myself. You can't take someone who has abused their body their whole life and change them overnight.

⊰⊱

I MET Duncan when I massaged him—sports massage, nothing kinky or weird. He said he fell in love with me right there and then.

His wife had not attended to him for years. They slept in separate rooms for the last five years of their marriage. He was so unhappy.

A lot of men asked me out after I massaged them—young men, too, footballers and all sorts. They'd get all turned on with the massage, you see, and with me being so attractive, they couldn't help themselves. I'd dated some, but mostly I had to behave like a professional and refuse. Usually, I didn't fancy them. But Duncan was different. He wooed me. It wasn't sleazy or anything like that. We were simply two people who fell in love, so I obliged him, of course, even at work.

Once he divorced and we married, he said he didn't want me working. I stopped, but I still treat myself to all the treatments. I've even resorted to Botox and fillers at my age. There is nothing worse than women heading to fifty and just giving up. My body is a temple.

I walk past the drinks' cabinet containing Duncan's alcohol. I hardly ever touch the stuff. Healthy is the only way to stay young and attractive, I remind myself, pouring kombucha. *Perhaps I'll flip through some of these magazines*, I think, staring out at the garden. The wind has blown a crisp packet into the flowerbeds. I sigh. I'll have to retrieve that now, and I still need to replace the vase in the hallway and put my glass away.

My work never stops.

⊰⊱

AS I LET the doggos out, I notice a green car pass, and then the police car again. The police have passed several times now. *How exciting!* I think for a moment, before remembering what trouble excitement can bring. I raise myself up to see where they might be heading. When they turn into my drive and get out of the car, I groan. A man and a woman cop. *Not another bloody murder!* It's turning into a joke around here now.

Realising some of the neighbours might be twitching their curtains, judging me, the murderer's sister, I get up and meet the bobbies at the door, carrying my glass, still in my pastel gym gear.

'Mrs. Whatmore? Lyssa Whatmore?'

'Yes,' I snap.

'Can we come in?'

I usher them in through to the kitchen, embarrassed by the wilting flowers. I will pop the vase back in position when I show them out. I'm multitasking, like any busy woman. I feel better now that the police are out of the gaze of the neighbours, but the car in the driveway is still a giveaway. Maybe there have been some break-ins.

'You might want to have seat?'

'No.' I pause. 'Why?'

'Please.'

It sounds like an order, not a request, so I perch on the bar stool.

'It's about your husband.'

I freeze, dropping my kombucha. The Edinburgh crystal glass shatters, leaving a lake of good gut health on the real slate flooring.

'There's a stray crisp packet in the hydrangeas I need to fetch,' I say, my voice wavering, as I stagger past them into the garden.

NINE

RHIANNON

'ARE you going to lift a manicured finger at all today, Debbie?' Preston huffs, his face twisting at the filth he has to work with.

He'd demanded a deep clean of the café as soon as he saw the state of it. Debbie had consented to him coming in on half wages to refurbish. She insisted she'd help. But she is not helping; instead, she sits on the bunker, checking her phone, as Preston, wearing marigold gloves, removes sludge from underneath the freezer units. He deposits the gunk into a bucket lump by lump.

Debbie sighs and puts her hands on the counter, as if to push herself down and attempt some work. Her phone rings at the same second, causing her to settle back down all over again.

I blow on my cappuccino, signifying I'm in no mood to help him out. Not my circus, not my monkeys. Debbie can only open for coffees until the refurb is finished and the inspectors are appeased. I don't normally patronise her café if I can help it, but seeing Debbie and Preston work together piqued my intrigue. It's every bit the fiasco I thought it would be.

'Hold on, Preston.' She lifts the phone to her ear. 'Hi ... Oh, she hung up.'

'Who was it?'

'Lyssa,' Debbie answers with a shrug. She remains on the counter, with no apparent intention of moving.

'Lyssa? Angela's sister?' Preston mumbles from beneath the counter.

'Yeah. She rang and then hung up.'

He pops his head out. 'Odd! Phone her back.'

I can see that Preston's love of intrigue and gossip overrides his need for Debbie to assist him. Or maybe he perceives the futility of that. Debbie stares at her phone in contemplation.

'She your pal then?' Preston ventures, after no movement from her.

'Kind of.' She pauses. 'She goes to the same tennis club, you know. We hang about in similar circles.' She flicks her hand.

Preston rolls his eyes as he returns to the depths of Debbie's units.

'She looks down on everyone, even me.'

'Even you! Wow!' responds Preston, his voice muffled from below. I giggle, but Debbie doesn't get the sarcasm.

'Everything's got to be the way she likes. It's either too this or too that. Nothing's ever right for bloody Goldilocks.'

Preston guffaws. For Debbie, that is quite witty.

'Honestly, I don't know why I'm friends with her anyway,' Debbie goes on. 'She's a sickening person. She lives in the best house up the hill. It's really old, but she's renovated inside, so it's as perfect as she is. I'll leave her. She can phone back if she wants me. I'm too busy.'

'Right enough, Debbie. You are fair run off your feet. Your plate is so full, it runneth over.' Preston titters at his own mangled idioms as he reverses out, stopping only when he notices Debbie isn't getting the joke. Heaving himself up, he takes the bucket outside. Debbie peers at its contents as he passes, her recoil gaining her a raised eyebrow from Preston.

'It's too tricky to reach to the back of the fridge units. I mean, who ever sees it?'

'It all needs pulled out. Come on, get on with it.' He indicates the bucket. 'If we both take an end of the handle, it'll be easy. It's not rocket surgery.'

Debbie fingers the handle, holding it as far away as possible. They make their way out to the car park.

'You can't hold your breath all the way there!' barks Preston.

'Ugh.' Debbie mutters.

I watch as they load the debris into a thick garbage bag and put it into the lined boot of the car.

'When the boot is full, we'll go up to the dump,' Preston instructs. 'It should take another half hour, I guess. Easy as falling off a piece of cake.'

'Do I have to go?' Debbie whines like a little girl.

'Yes! It's your muck!' To placate her, he adds, 'We can take a gander at the garden centre after. You like Strawberry Corner, right?' Her face brightens at the prospect of a retail experience.

Debbie's phone rings again.

'Hi, Lyssa,' Debbie answers this time, miming to Preston, 'It's Lyssa.'

'Never!'

'Yeah, I missed your call, or you hung up or something. Not sure what...' A gasp escapes her.

What?' Preston mouths.

'Uh-huh. Oh God, no!'

'What?' Preston gesticulates for her explain. Debbie flaps him away, shaking her head and walking round the car park in circles, her face losing all colour.

'Where? OK, right. I'm down at the café. I'll be five minutes.'

'No!' Preston mimes.

Hanging up, she spins to face him. 'Preston, we need to leave it.'

'Oh, for effs sake Debbie.' Preston moans. She snatches her bag and throws it over her shoulder.

'What is it? What's happened?' I ask, finally giving up my bystander status.

'Can't say.'

'Why? What about the dump?' Preston adds.

'Empty the car boot out. I need to go!'

'Why? What is it?'

'A bloody nightmare, that's what! Poor Lyssa!'

TEN

LYSSA

Twenty minutes earlier

THE POLICEWOMAN FOLLOWS me into the garden and stops me with a gentle touch to my arm. I stand shaking, shivering, staring at the crisp packet in the flower bed, or somewhere beyond it at nothing at all. My legs give way from the shock. I black out.

Eventually, I come round on the grass. 'I've been fasting for eighteen hours, part of my intermittent fasting regime—one of my diets. I read about it in one of my magazines.' Then I remember where I am and who I'm talking to. 'I don't understand what's happening,' I murmur, as the policeman helps me up. He leads me back into the house with a strong arm, settling me down on the sofa in the living room. I assume he fears I'll fall off the bar stool in the kitchen. He leaves me with the woman while he fetches a glass of water.

I balance it on the chair arm, my hand still quivering.

'Your husband has been found dead,' the policewoman reminds me. 'We believe he suffered a heart attack.'

'Oh no.' *What else can be said?*

'I'm afraid so.'

'In his hotel room?' I hear myself ask, although it doesn't feel like me voicing the words.

'It's ... delicate,' says the policewoman, glancing at her colleague.

He licks his lips and then tightens them as he stares at the floor. I wonder if he needs the water I'm gripping. *Why am I thinking about that while my husband lies dead?*

I sense anxiety in both officers. It's understandable. It must be a difficult job, delivering news of a sudden death.

'He ... he was getting a massage,' the policewoman stutters. 'He'd had a massage and been left to relax, and then the ... erm ... girl... came back in and found him dead.'

'In the spa?' I know there is a spa in the hotel he uses in Saudi. 'We always book a spa hotel when we go on holiday to Spain, Dubai or anywhere,' I babble on.

She stops me with a fixed look.

What am I twittering on about holidays for? Am I here? Are the police sitting there?

I stare at the John Lewis cushions and then back towards the police officers. They are still there. I blink hard and then open my eyes wide. *Still there.* I stick my new gel nails into my hand to feel pain, to prove I'm still awake. *This is happening in real life.*

The nervous policeman leans forward and takes the glass of water off me. I assume he needs a drink, but then I notice I'm sitting at a precarious angle. I guess he thought I'd let that tip. He already cleared up the kombucha mess in kitchen. Maybe that's why he looks so anxious.

'Saudi?' he asks.

'Yes. He's in Saudi at the moment. He's very important in the bomb disposal field.'

The two of them exchange glances.

'He was in ... G-Geylang,' the man stammers, looking at his notes. 'Where?'

'Geylang, Singapore,' the policewoman clarifies.

'Singapore?' I question.

'Singapore.'

'Singapore?' I repeat.

'Singapore!' The policewoman barks slightly to jolt me out of this verbal tennis.

'I don't understand.' I feel as if I might stop breathing.

'Your husband was in Singapore, in a massage ... erm ... parlour.'

'Brothel,' snaps the policeman. The woman widens her eyes and glares at him. He must think bluntness is the best path at this point. I'm clearly not getting it.

My leg starts twitching up and down, out of my control, as if it is someone else's.

'No.' I utter.

'Is there anyone you can call to sit with you?' the woman asks.

'My sister.'

'OK, your sister.'

'No, no, no, no! Not my sister. Not my sister.' I jump up, feeling my face contort as much as my fresh Botox will let it. Maria, my beautician, told me not to do that, but it can't be helped. 'I forgot. My sister is dead.' I sit down, lightheaded again. 'My sister is dead,' I whisper, feeling my lips wobble.

'Sorry to hear that,' comments the policeman. The woman throws him another look.

'My sister is dead, and now my husband is dead!' The words come out of my mouth in a contorted wail. 'I don't have anyone.'

'We don't want to leave you alone with this ... news. Are there any children that could come?' He gestures toward the photos in the hall.

'They aren't mine. Surely you don't think I look old enough to have children that age.' I bite. 'They're his children...! Oh God, I'll need to tell them, too.'

'Well, we must have someone with you. It is a terrible shock.'

I grasp my phone. I can't focus for the tears in my eyes. I don't feel like I'm crying, but my eyes are wet. My hands shake as I struggle to dial. 'Debbie. I'll call Debbie.'

They watch in silence as I ring my solitary friend. Then I cancel the call. 'No, I can't. I can't say he was in a massage parlour in Singapore!'

They say nothing momentarily.

'There's something else... The lady in question ...' ventures the policeman.

'Lady, huh? Oh, some lady. Who cares about her?' I half laugh.

The woman takes over. 'She claims to be his wife.'

'What?'

'We wonder if perhaps there may be confusion in translation.'

'Of course, there is! She's a money-grabbing hooker.' I pull the tassel off the cushion I didn't realise I was gripping.

'The authorities are making further enquiries.'

'Perhaps he was there so often that she said he was her husband,' adds the policeman. Side-eyeing the man, the policewoman unclenches her teeth enough to add, 'You should call your friend.'

'And tell her all that?'

'You don't need to tell her everything. Just the basics,' the policewoman suggests.

'No, right. Right, no one can know. OK.' I dial again.

'Debs. Hi! I have no one else to call.' I wasn't going to have Debbie think she was *that* important. 'Hi, Debs. Listen. Duncan is dead, and the police are here.' I glance at them. 'Um ... he had a heart attack.' I pause. 'Where? Where?' I glance at the policeman again, and then breathe in and straighten up. I harden my face, not taking my eyes of them. 'Abroad. Working. Uh-huh. Uh-huh. Yes, Debbie.' I hang up. 'She ... she is coming over. She'll be five minutes. I'll phone Greg, too.'

'Who is Greg?'

'Greg Holstead. Duncan's friend. Erm, solicitor.'

'OK.'

'Yes, he'll know what to do. He'll fix this mess.' I find Greg's number. I am breathing easier now. Anger is staring to trump shock. 'Oh God ... the answering machine,' I say to the police, covering the mouthpiece. 'Hi, Greg. It's Lyssa. Duncan ... just, just.' I can't bring myself to say it again, especially to a machine. 'It's an emergency. A dire emergency. Call me when you can or come to the house right away.'

I turn to the police again and pull myself together. 'You can go now. I'll get everything sorted out. I've had a shock, and there's been a huge misunderstanding.' I sniff, take a deep breath, and smile. 'I'll see you out.' I haven't forgotten to be a good hostess.

As they leave, Debbie races up, kisses me on both cheeks and wails, 'Darling!'

ELEVEN

RHIANNON

'DID you see her at the funeral?' Preston blurts out, bursting through the door.

'Who?' I'm startled, assuming I've missed something or someone important.

'Lyssa!' he announces, barging past me with his shopping. It's hardly the revelation his dramatics are painting.

'Of course. I spoke to her. You saw me. So did you.' I rise to help him. *I mean is that it?*

'White-blonde hair on her, nothing like Angie.' He doesn't stop talking, nor unpacking. Continuing to empty the bags onto the counter, he then swivels to face me. 'Angela had brown hair. Aye, that's right, *brown*.' He returns to his business, as if his point has been made.

I am none the wiser. 'What?' I question.

'What was she like at school?'

'Angela?'

'No! Lyssa,' he hisses. He does an about face.

I lift the lid of the tea bag tin and fill it with new bags.

'Hair wise?' he adds, to clarify.

This conversation still makes little sense to me. I can't imagine Debbie would have left the café in such a flap just to help Lyssa dye her hair.

'She had brown hair at school. Lighter than Angela's, but brown,' I answer the question. 'Light brown.'

He appears triumphant. 'Aye. I reckoned the curtains didnae match the carpet.'

I snort, as we trudge on with our mundane tasks. 'Any more news about today?'

He halts his work and folds his arms. 'Well, something has happened. An emergency.'

Honestly. 'Yes. What kind of emergency, Preston?'

'No idea what is going on, but I'm damn sure I'll find out. In fact, I'll text her now.' He mouths every syllable of his text. 'Ev-er-y-thing O-K? Hash-tag. Con-cerned. Brid-ge Street. Question mark. I tell you, I'm asking Calum Grant next time I'm in getting my hair done,' he adds.

'What about?'

'Lyssa's hair.'

'He'll not tell you. He's bound to confidentiality.'

'Is not. He's no' a priest or a dentist. He's no' signed a hypocritic oaf or anything!'

'Hippocratic oath.'

'Aye, what I said!' A single breath in, he shuts the fridge door and announces, 'Right, I'm away out. I've tickets to a Meatloaf tribute act.'

'Is that your kind of thing?'

'Not really, but my friend is the act. Sounds exactly like him.'

'Yeah?'

'Aye, looks like him, too—sitting down.' He smirks, leaning against the door frame.

'How sitting down?' I'm like a fish being reeled in.

'He's quite short. Five foot one.'

'Oh. How tall was Meatloaf?'

'A good six-footer!'

'Oh, I didn't realise he was so tall. So your mate is a foot shorter?'

'Aye. We got around it, though. I came up with his tribute name.'

'What's that?'

He pops a wrapper in the bin on his way out. With a slam of the bin lid, he retorts, 'Half Loaf.' Then he whirls around and leaves. His chuckle floats from the vicinity of the flat stairs until the front door slams. 'See ya later!'

TWELVE

LYSSA

'I'LL NEED to break into the office,' Greg says, pushing his shoulder against the door. Even with all his considerable strength from those gym work outs I see him doing, it doesn't give way like it would in the movies.

'The den,' I correct.

'The what?' He snaps, but then he follows in a gentler manner, 'Yes, the den.' Turning to me, he asks, 'Would Duncan have all his documentation in here? There's nowhere else?' He tries another futile attempt at the handle.

'Let me move the dogs. They are getting upset.'

He looks at them snapping around his ankles, but he does not react except to say, 'I don't mind dogs. They've an unshakable loyalty that I like.'

'Yes, yes,' I mutter, unsure where he's going with that comment. 'You are very patient.' I shove my doggos in the living room and shut the door. 'Right. Anyway, he kept everything in his office, but I'm not allowed to go in there,' I explain.

'I think we can safely go in now!' Greg says, adding a quick, 'Sorry.'

'I don't know where the key is.'

'I'll call a locksmith. I know a guy.' He dials the number.

'What are we looking for?'

'Any documents. A life insurance policy. His copy of the will, mainly. Or any more up-to-date versions I'm not aware of. I'll have the original at the office, barring any new ones he might have made?'

It sounds like a question

'I doubt he would have made another—'

'—without me?'

'Without you, Greg.'

'I'll be the executor of his will. I have no doubt.'

'Yes. I guess so.'

'And ...' He strokes the door frame. 'I can check if there is—How can I put this?—anything related to this woman.'

I flinch.

'What do you know already?' He has the gall to ask me to my face.

'I don't know anything much. There's a woman who claims she's his wife. It's all ridiculous, of course—some whore after his money, but it all needs sorted out, and I don't know how to.'

'I'll contact the foreign office and find out what is going on. I'll take care of it. There must have been a mistake. Some people say wife when they mean mistress. It may have been lost in translation.'

'That's what the police said.' I slump against the wall. 'Oh God, I can't face this, Greg.'

The locksmith answers just at that minute. Greg puts his hand on my shoulder.

'Hi, I need into a room,' Greg tells them. 'We've lost the key. No, it's a client's room. I'm her solicitor. It's not to the house. It's a locked room in the house. Her deceased husband's office.' He whispers to me, 'Have a seat. I'm used to this,' as he leads me through to the couch. 'You can? Yes, it is an emergency. Not life and death, but we do need in ASAP.'

Greg pours me a large, neat brandy and orders me to down it. I'm asleep in no time at all.

⁎

I WAKE COVERED IN A THROW, with Greg sitting at the end of the couch. 'Oh, Greg. How long have I been asleep?' I sit up. 'Did you get in? Did you find what you needed?'

'I found the life insurance. There are no other wills in there, but for some reason, his copy isn't there either. I must have given him one. Could it be anywhere else?'

'No, I don't deal with anything. Greg, is there anything about her in the will? The one you have?'

'I haven't looked it out yet.'

'But you must remember.'

'I can't recall. It could have been years since he updated it. I deal with thousands of wills. It may have been arranged, I don't know, fifteen or twenty years ago.'

'But ...'

'Lyssa, I can't tell you. I don't remember, but I will search it out as soon as I get back to the office. Don't worry.'

'What about the funeral? What about his body?'

'I'll deal with the foreign office. You either arrange to have the funeral overseas or for the body to be returned to the UK.'

'UK, of course.'

'So, repatriation. If you wish the funeral to be held in the UK, you have to use international undertakers. Before you can bring his body home, you'll need a certified English translation of the foreign death certificate from Singapore. Leave that to me. You need authorisation to remove his body from the country. As his wife, you will have no problem getting this.'

'Unless this woman ...?'

'I know. It's another hurdle. But we'll clear that up and get the ball rolling. Lie back down and have a rest. I'll see my own way out.'

I fall asleep again. Later, I wake, drink some water, and take a pill for my banging headache. I never drink brandy. I shower, a long shower. And as I come out, the phone rings.

'Greg here, Lyssa.'

'Hi.'

'Lyssa, I'll need you to come into the office.'

'Why?'

'Erm, there's an issue you need to know about.'

'Tell me now.'

'No. I need to be with you for this.' He hangs up.

THIRTEEN

RHIANNON

'OH MY GOD,' I hear Preston exclaim from the vicinity of the café outhouse as I exit my car. I often hear him before I see him.

'It's a bit of a dump, I'm afraid.' It seems Debbie is there, too.

'You hit the nail right on the nose there, Debbie,' Preston says as I round the corner to view the scene.

'Bloody hell,' I say out loud.

Debbie curls her lip.

'It's almost as bad as the café itself.' Preston hoots.

'Ha ha, very funny!' Debbie sneers, adding, 'Hi, Rhiannon,' as an afterthought.

'Hiya, Debbie. Preston, I take it you aren't ready to go?' I ask. He'd promised to accompany me to visit Mum in the care home after his work here. Having company always makes the visits easier, and Preston never lets a conversation run dry.

'Erm, actually. I've not long arrived myself. I got a wee bit held up on the way.'

'You left two hours ago!' I whine.

'You know me. I can hardly get along the street without meeting somebody. What did you say this was, Debbie? The outhouse?'

'A storeroom most recently, but it's been empty for years. It was a wee house until they renovated the bakery into the café. This whole place is ancient. Maybe the baker lived in parts of it, but it's been empty for yonks. I heard they kept chickens in it at one time.'

'Beautiful,' Preston replies, scrunching up his nose. 'Well, I'll fix it up, but you'll need more staff in to cover the general cleaning in the café.'

'I'll get Rough in.'

'I beg your pardon?'

'Rough! Julie! Also known as Rough—short for Rough-as-guts.'

'Fabulous. She sounds ideal,' Preston replies sarcastically,

I cough for attention.

'Have a wee cappuccino again, Rhiannon. You like those. I'll do an hour, hour and a half tops today.' He adds hopefully, 'Or you could grab an end ...' and gestures at the mess before him.

I roll my eyes and trudge off to fetch my coffee. I'll take a biscuit too. One of the good ones. There is no danger of me lifting a finger. When I return, they haven't either.

'Just some stuff from those boxes and tools and bits. It's pretty much empty,' Preston muses out loud.

'Apart from the mice,' Debbie adds. One scuttles along the floor, causing Preston to flinch. I perch on the wall and place my feet on an upturned crate to use as a stool, out the way of any passing vermin.

'What is the big plan, Debs?'

'Right, the new hatch for serving at night will open up here, on this wall,' she explains, pointing. 'So we don't need to open the café and have all the drunks causing a riot at night. They can access the hatch by the alley.'

Preston nods, understanding. 'So, you want it to be a shell to start with?'

'Aye.'

'OK. We'll do the clearing part today.'

Debbie doesn't move to help. Neither do I. I sip my coffee. My irritation about being delayed is lessened knowing my visiting time with Mum is being eaten into through no fault of my own. Now, I can observe this pantomime in amusement.

'OK? Well, we could stand here and talk until the cows turn blue, but we need to get stuck in,' Preston says, lifting a box to hand to Debbie. She keeps her hands by her sides and recoils at the dust. He pushes past her, tutting. Entering the building again, he indicates upwards. I peer in.

'What's that?'

'The ceiling, obviously.' Debbie shrugs.

'A false ceiling, by the looks of it. It's all rotten. It will need to go.'

'Fair enough.'

Preston pokes it with a broom.

'So, what's the craic with Lyssa? You looked white as a sheet when she called yesterday, and you never answered my text.'

'Her husband died.'

'Jeez! What?' I splutter, choking on my drink. 'Oh my God. No!'

'Yeah, he was ... um ... working abroad.'

'Oh God, what a shocker. How old was he?'

'Sixty-two ... and ...' Debbie stammers.

'And?'

'Oh, nothing.'

'Don't leave me hanging,' Preston warns, still bashing away at the ceiling.

'So ...' Debbie begins and then exclaims, 'Oh!' as a portion of the ceiling collapses. They manage to dodge most of it, but dust and debris flies everywhere, covering their clothes and hair.

Fabulous. I'm glad I came. I grab my phone to take a photo. This is priceless.

'Are you joking, Preston? I just had my hair done this morning!' Debbie moans, shaking herself down.

'What's that?' they both say together, spotting something new. They peer at another part of the ceiling. My interest piqued, I join them inside. Preston brushes it with the broom, revealing a hatch.

'There's a catch there!'

'Unlock it!' I demand.

'A secret compartment!' Preston reaches up. 'Finders keepers, by the way,' he adds. 'Especially if it's a stash of cash.'

'Ha! I own the building, thank you very much, and everything in it.' Debbie shakes her head at him.

'Fair enough. You go get it, then!' He huffs and folds his arms.

'Get it, please Preston,' she whines in her little girl voice.

He sighs, as he reaches up. 'I bet you it's full of mice, or maybe a rat!' He undoes the catch and allows the inverted trap door to fall. Strips of material dangle from the ceiling.

'Weird,' he says, poking at them with the broom. 'The material is wrapped around something in there.'

'Pull them off,' Debbie orders.

'Yes, boss! But before I do, how much are you paying me for this? What if it's a body?'

'Get on with it!' I demand.

'OK, I've got it.' Preston picks and pulls until more material frees.

A wooden, board-like object appears beneath the swaddles of rag. Preston lifts the large rectangular object out onto the floor and perches it on the boxes. 'What are those? Clothes?'

'No, they're flags. Like bunting. Old Bunting the moths have chewed,' I say. 'But what's underneath?'

He peels back the flag material, unwrapping the object halfway and laying it against the wall for Debbie to see.

We all shuffle back to view it.

Preston gawps until his mouth shapes the words, 'What the hell?'

FOURTEEN

LYSSA

I ARRIVE at Greg's dimly lit work premises and try the door. Locked. The reception area beyond the large shop window is in darkness, although light emanates from a back room.

Why would Greg tell me to meet him here at this hour? I glance behind me to the dark street. The odd car drives past, although rush hour is over. I knock on the door, then spin to scan the street. I spy a solo dog walker, two youths lurking by the corner shop, and a slight chap with a baseball cap sitting in a car nearby. The dancing light from the phone screen he is fixated on catches my eye. I wonder what he's up to, until the street becomes a sudden hive of activity, with cars arriving from all directions. The church doors open to a bright light, and children flock out. Parents are thrown bags and crafts from the youth club and juggle them back into their cars.

My attention is diverted from the Bridge Street happenings by a harassed-looking secretary opening the door.

'At last,' I groan.

'We're closed. I'm just leaving,' she snips, not shifting.

What's her problem?

'Thanks,' a voice comes from behind her. 'I'll see this lady.'

It's Greg.

She looks me up and down before shifting out of the doorway, sniffing and folding her arms. Her handbag, propped on her shoulder, drops to her elbow, but her eyes never leave me. Women often treat me like that. I'm used to it. It's jealousy. She is plain—I'm not. She's older than me, to begin with, just a couple years off being a haggard crone. She would have been an attractive woman once, but the bags under her eyes drag her down. I had my eyes lifted two years ago, taking at least a decade off.

'Come in, come in,' Greg's welcoming tone cuts through the frosty atmosphere.

She holds back, watching me enter. Even once I'm in the building, I find myself pinned by her stare. For someone who was just leaving, she is remarkably motionless.

'Thanks. That's all,' Greg states more firmly, ushering her by the elbow out the door. She shrugs off his touch. After throwing him a look, she flings her bag over her shoulder and slams the door on her way out.

She needs sacking, I think. *He must be more assertive with his staff.* We both watch, for some reason, as she crosses the road.

With her out of sight, Greg springs into action, stepping forward to click the latch. He smiles a thin-lipped smile and shrugs, offering no explanation for his huffy secretary. Pivoting, he indicates the door to the well-lit back room and I lead the way to his office.

'Sorry it's so late, but I considered it best to deal with this as soon as possible,' he says, making his way to the leather chair on the far side of the desk.

I nod and sit on the plastic client's seat. It feels small and is lower than his, as I sit awaiting an explanation.

'I think it's best not to prolong these things. It saves further worry,' he says, settling into his comfy leather seat.

It is reassuring to me that I am here so he can put my mind at ease. 'Thank you. You and your receptionist are working late.' I turn to look where I came in, as if she might have returned.

'She was working late. I had gone out for a walk, but I came back in so we could have this chat. I expected her to have gone home. She has worked here a long time, you understand.' He makes small talk, shuffling his papers, and I join in chatting to fill the silence. I'm good at that. I always was with my clients, too.

'I sobered up from that brandy.' I find I've lost my ability to talk about the weather, holidays, and other pointless nonsense. I drop my head and manage to blurt out 'Your shoes are all muddy.'

'Uh-huh. As I said, I've been on a walk. I always take a drive and then a stroll by the river at the end of the working day. I've a boat ...' Greg tapers off. 'I'm going to cut to the chase, Lyssa. I've called the foreign office and sought out the will from our files.'

'Okay.'

'First things first.' He purses his lips and then continues. 'Kwai Tan, the woman who claims to be Duncan's wife.'

'Kwai what?'

'Kwai Tan.'

'You know her name?'

'Yes. The woman who reported Duncan's death is Kwai Tan, from ...' He checks his notes and enunciates each syllable, 'the Geylang province of Singa-pore. A poor neighbourhood, I'm told.' He pauses and inhales. Then he holds in another breath before releasing it.

Silence.

'It turns out she is legally married to Duncan in Singapore,' he blurts out. 'She has the marriage certificate.'

'Fake!' I cry, as soon as Greg finishes his sentence.

His lips purse again. 'I'm afraid not,' he says after a pause. I have checked with the authorities there. It is all recorded legally in Singapore. It's in the official records.'

I feel sick. *How can this be happening?*

'But *I'm* his wife. Everyone knows I'm Duncan Whatmore's wife! He's married her bigamously!'

Our lapse in conversation is broken only by Greg tapping his pen on the desk. It bothers me. My eyes land on it, tip-tapping up and down on the green leather desk surface. I yearn to grab it and throw it across the room. I never behave like that, nor even think that way. My angry sister flits through my mind. *What if I'm like her? Angry Angela.* It makes me wonder what I am capable of.

'Erm, no. I'm afraid they married prior to your wedding to Duncan. I have the documents here.' He lifts a folder. I stare at it, as he continues. 'She is his legal wife. Technically, you are not married. You and Duncan only had a ceremony. He bigamously married you, as you might put it.' As if to put a full stop to his statements, he adds, 'I'm afraid you are not legally his wife.'

FIFTEEN

LYSSA

SPEECHLESS, I focus on the papers that have thrown my life into turmoil. Greg's pen-tapping has stopped at least, although he is talking again.

'It means she is legally able to keep him—I mean … his body—in Singapore and bury him there. She has the legal right to hold a funeral for him. Singaporean authorities confirmed those are her wishes. She has no desire to repatriate him to Scotland.'

'Good God! Everyone will be expecting him to be buried at Inveresk,' I say, my voice raising in pitch and volume as my throat tightens. 'The neighbours will ask questions!'

His eyebrows lower into a furrow. 'And that explains the will.' He holds up a second folder. 'I looked out the will, and he has left her everything.'

'What? Because *she* is his wife?'

'Yes. And she is named so in the will. Seems he arranged it after he married her. He did not update it with us after he met you. I could not find another will in the den, as you called it. Nor even a copy of the one I have here. Do you know where that might be? Is there anywhere else that it could be kept?'

'I don't deal with paperwork!' I bite

'Never mind. The main thing is: there is no more recent will naming you as inheriting anything.'

'You ... you must have known about this!' I am the one in the dark, and everyone else must have known. Life feels dangerous and unpredictable.

'I guess I forgot.'

'You forgot?' I half-laugh.

'I forgot. It was years ago. Decades. I couldn't recall, but I have the will here in black and white. Unless another will turns up, Kwai Tan is Duncan's main beneficiary.'

'Main?'

'It leaves each of his children a lump sum.'

I feel a surge of adrenaline. 'Jack and Carol.'

'And the child he shares with Kwai Tan.'

I'm so jittery, I could be physically sick. 'And the house?'

'I'm afraid it is Kwai Tan's house now.'

'This cannot be happening.' I'm surprised to hear myself say it out loud, although it has been running through my mind for the past ten minutes.

'I'm so sorry, Lyssa.'

'What will *she* do with a house in Scotland?' I am scrabbling about for some hope.

'I don't know for sure. As executor of the will, I have to deal with her now regarding this. She has been advised to contact me directly.'

I can't swallow. I feel like I'm going to drown in my own saliva. An ear-piercing squeal sounds in my ears, as Greg rambles on.

'I will arrange for the money to be transferred to her to pay for the funeral. As I'm the only solicitor she will know in this country, and Duncan's executor, I will work with her to arrange the house sale.'

'House sale?'

'I imagine so.'

'And where does this leave me? The life insurance?'

'There is a glimmer of hope there. You are named as a beneficiary in his life insurance. There should be no problem with that, but I'll need to double check.' His head drops as he makes notes.

'Don't I have any rights?'

He looks up and shakes his head. 'Do you have any money in your own name? There is a joint account I saw amongst ...' He fumbles with his papers

'Yes.'

'You are entitled to any money in the joint account, and, of course, your own possessions and your own money. I doubt Kwai Tan ...' He trails off again, probably seeing my glare at the name of a woman I had never heard of until today.

'I doubt she will want furniture, used furniture etcetera, from a foreign country.'

'Good God. Oh no, she won't want my cast-offs.' I look around for someone to tell me this is one huge joke.

'Are you able to afford to live for now?' he asks.

'I'll be down to my last, I don't know, maybe four hundred and fifty thousand until the insurance money comes in.' My chest tightens. I feel like I want to run, so I stand up to leave. There's nothing more to say.

Twice in two days I have felt this way. My usual positive thinking tells me to believe that the stress and increased adrenaline will burn up more calories. *Look on the bright side of everything.* But it's not right. It's not the time. I can't think this way today.

I stagger out of the solicitor's office with the realisation that I am now homeless.

SIXTEEN

RHIANNON

TWO EYES PEEP out from a thick layer of grime covering a large oil painting in a gilt frame. Preston, Debbie and I stare at the object propped against the hen house wall. Preston ventures forward, carefully chipping away like an archaeologist at the remaining yellowed flags that have been the painting's bed for so many years. I join him. Preston and I flick away more dust and mouse droppings to show the complete face and torso of a lady. The painting depicts her sitting from the waist up. The lady wears a chain. Preston follows the line of the chain down.

'What's that?' he whispers to me.

'I can't tell.'

He pushes away more grime.

'The bottom half of the picture has rotted,' he says.

'Damaged by years of attrition, erosion, and abrasion. No matter how much care is taken, age and time take their toll, and we all turn to dust,' I add, dramatically.

'Very poetic. But it's the mice more likely.' Debbie rolls her eyes. Her arms remain folded, avoiding the dirt despite her already dusty hair.

'Aye, the ones that gnawed at the flags,' Preston says matter-of-factly.

'Who put this here, though? And why?' My eyes are transfixed on the woman's face.

Peeling back the flags further, Preston reveals her old-fashioned dress, a ruffled blouse poking up from her stiff, black-corseted bodice.

'Look for anything on it!' demands Preston.

'Like?' questions Debbie.

'A date or a painter's name.' I push past her and grab the artwork, blowing some more dust and debris from its surface, while turning it in every direction. 'Nothing to see. The artist might have signed it near the bottom, but it's nibbled at down there.'

'Then who is she? It's a mystery! It's not like anyone poor could afford that sort of thing! Like, "I'll be late back tonight. I'm away down the pit now, but I'm getting my portrait done on my way home."'

Debbie snorts at Preston's suggestion.

'She's all in black, a widow?' I suggest.

'A lonely, desperate widow,' Preston agrees, his head tilted to the side.

'Quite pretty, if a bit fat,' Debbie adds.

That breaks Preston out of his whimsy. 'For fuck's sake, Debbie, no' everyone is trying to be a middle-aged spice girl.'

'She's got a sweet smile,' I add.

'Yes.'

'But a stupid haircut.' Debbie contributes.

'It was probably the height of fashion in eighteen hundred something.' Preston snaps, defending his new friend.

'She's bound to have lived up the hill in Inveresk, no doubt.'

'Turn it over, Rhiannon!' Preston demands. 'There might be an address of the framer or something.

I scan the painting again, but on the other side this time.

'There's something written in the top corner in pencil. It's quite faded.' I push my specs to the end of my nose. 'W.O. My love forever P.T. 1848,' I read aloud.

'Ooh, a love token,' Debbie coos.

'Jesus, you cannae put that in a locket!' Preston screeches. 'Fecking size of the thing. Ha!' The lady is almost life-sized.

'But why was she hidden?' Debbie questions. Her phone buzzes, drawing her attention away.

'An illicit affair no doubt, the dirty buggers!' Preston squeals 'But who is W.O.? Who is P.T.? And how is it here?'

'The baker's shop was named Thomson's before I bought it. That might fit the T.'

'Was it always called Thomson's, this place?' I question. Without waiting for an answer, I continue, 'I'll find out. I'll ask on the Facebook page.'

I retrieve my phone from the wall and search the 'Musselburgh Folks' page on Facebook. Usually dedicated to local missing cats and to moaning about the council, this might be a refreshing change. I read aloud as I type. 'Was Debbie's café always Thomson's the bakers before? And how long ago was it called that?' Then to Preston, I say, 'Let's see how far they can go back.'

'Ask if they know the baker's name!' Preston pipes up.

'Edit: Also, what was Thomson the baker's first name? And any other bakers before him?'

'Could you look at the deeds or somewhere else?' Preston suggests. 'Like historical documents and things like that.'

'Good idea, Inspector Clouseau.' My phone pings, interrupting me, and I open up the app. 'Patrick Thomson and his dad owned the shop. His grandad and great grandad were also Patricks.'

'Bloody hell, they had little imagination,' Preston chips in, rolling his eyes.

'Not everyone names their kids weird names, Preston.'

'Did I tell you I have a sister called Valencia?'

'Yes! And other lies!'

'Well, that was easy enough. Patrick Thomson, we'll go with that. Who is W? Wilma? Winifred? Wilhelmina?'

'Or ... Wynona.' Debbie butts in, looking up from her phone.

'Get a grip, Debbie. Its East Lothian you reside in, no' Hollywood.' Preston guffaws. Then he pauses and stares at the painting again. He folds his arms in determination. 'We'll away search online about Pat-a-Cake the baker's man. Then let's see if we can find a connection to W! I think we'll also need to get someone official to look at this painting. It could be worth a lot of dosh.'

Debbie steps forwards and lifts the lady. 'OK. Let me take her out and put her in the back of the shop for now. You carry on here for a bit with the clearing out, will you? I need to go see Lyssa. It's a disaster. She just texted. The house needs to go up for sale or something. I'll leave all the investigating to you two.'

'Okay, we'll get on it. I'll add to my big list of to-do's.'

'Do it! Do all of that,' she orders, heading out back to the café.

'Say hiya to Lyssa for me,' Preston yells, and then mutters to me, as he surveys the mysterious lady once more. 'Poor lassie is going to hell in a handbag,'

SEVENTEEN

LYSSA

I DON'T FEEL SINGLE; instead, I feel I'm now half of a couple. A halfuple. A solo voice in a duet. I looked at the letters of confirmation of my non-marriage from the meeting from Greg and shouted, 'I am still a wife!'

Driving home from booking Inveresk Church for his memorial service yesterday, I'd thought *I must tell Duncan about the arrangements*. How stupid is that?

It's so not like me to feel this unsettled. I know Duncan died, but I don't believe it. In the car, I said his name out loud over and over. 'Duncan, Duncan, Duncan, Duncan, Duncan.' Louder and louder, until I was shouting. I needed to say it several times. I'd saved up his name because I can't say it to his face or summon him with a call from the kitchen. I've no reason to say his name at all these days. But everyone knows I'm Lyssa Whatmore, and I'm not changing that! Duncan died, but our relationship outlives him. I carry his name like a trademark. I'll be named as his wife at the memorial.

The minister has agreed not to go into the gory details. I'm faking it until I make it. If you say your version of the truth enough, those who don't know will believe it. Others who know the truth forget in time. *It's all about attitude,* I remind myself, sitting up straighter.

AS I'D WALKED out of the van onto the street yesterday, I'd looked up to see my husband walking towards me. Part of my brain collected information about the face in front of me and assessed the clothing and gait as Duncan's. Another part had fired in a different direction, asking questions.

It can't be him.

Why is he here?

I'd smiled at the apparition, but it didn't see me, just as a ghost might not. He walked right past. It was simply a man who looked a little like Duncan, which left me deflated. But I know I will look for that man every day, hoping he might walk by.

Is it surprising that I'm sad and grieving Duncan? After all, he lied to me. He cheated. He left me in this terrible situation. Many would assume I'd feel happy he died, the bastard. But the pain doesn't stop me longing for him. I miss our social events: Tennis club, bridge, and charity galas. I even miss his mess, his snoring, his talking, his singing, and his TV blaring. I miss his banging around in his den, his presence in the house—even when I could not see or hear him. My bed was often half-empty at night, and again when I woke up in the morning, as Duncan was away working so often. I am used to being alone. It makes this more difficult to comprehend.

It is easier for me to forget I am a widow. I don't feel like he has died most of the time. Even when he worked away, I knew he existed somewhere. He still lives in my head, making guest appearances in my dreams, making waking up even more difficult. I can't take in that now he isn't *anywhere.* I scour our text messages and email threads. I listen to his voicemail on repeat. His voice haunts the room.

'Leave a message and I'll call you back,' he promises. I am tempted, but I click it off instead. I call again a few minutes later.

I scroll through his Facebook page, and anyone associated with him, for glimpses of his life.

Who was this man I married?

No, not married—the man I had a ceremony with.

I spot his daughter, Carol, on a trip to Singapore twenty years ago.

Is that a fascinator on her head in that photo? I feel my throat tighten.

Oh my God! Did she know? Was she there at their wedding? She wasn't invited to ours, and she never said anything. I try to recall. *When was I last there?*

Eight years ago, we visited Singapore for a few days on a stop over to Australia. I remember Duncan said he needed to attend a meeting one day. A friend of his lived there at the time, and their meeting in Saudi had been postponed. He said it was so opportune they could catch up and save rescheduling. He left me with his credit card and insisted I go shopping. I bought a bag and a scarf. He was gone a whole day.

A whole day! Where was he? Where was the meeting? Who was he meeting? He was with her!

I go to my closet and find the box marked scarves. *Where is it?* I scrabble and curse until I find it. *My whole life was a lie.* I am suddenly livid. I blame myself for trusting the wrong person. *But how can that be? I'm full of so much positive energy! Positive things should come to me!* It frustrates me further. I don't know how I brought this on myself. Maybe I have been doing it all wrong.

There it is! I take the scarf to the kitchen and start cutting it up. I rip it into shreds until I see blood dripping onto the floor. I have cut my hand. I start to cry. *I have brought this on myself, too.* But I can't understand how.

I still want him back. I still want him and everything back as it should be. I want it back how it never really was.

EIGHTEEN

RHIANNON

'MAKE WAY, make way! Someone moving in!' Preston exclaims, tearing into the living room. He spins around, heading back out the door along the corridor to our bedrooms, which both overlook the street.

'Moving in where?' I haul myself up from the sofa before he has a chance to answer. I guess that, whoever they are, they're moving into these flats. I race to follow him into his room.

'See!' Preston points.

A frown settles on my face as I spy a removal van outside. 'To what flat? And who?'

'Upstairs! Into Angela's old gaff. Callum's place. I followed a fellow with a lampstand up to the landing.'

'There was a guy in there last week.'

'Callum's pal left. He was only staying for a wee while, rent-free.'

'I can't keep up.'

'Who's that?' He points again.

'Where?'

'There! Rocking up behind them. Is that *Angela's* van?' he questions, as the driver jumps down from the front seat. Preston blusters, contorting his body to view the scene. 'I can't see from here. Some young lassie?' He bends down and pulls on his trainers.

'It's not a young lassie. It's Alyssa. I mean *Lyssa*.'

He takes another look. 'Oh, so it is. How are you two the same age? I'm away down to investigate.'

I UNDERSTAND. He means I look older. She's all smoke and mirrors, with her hair done and make-up and fillers. She's slim like me, but I'm scrawnier. I check myself in Preston's mirror. *Ugh, my roots need done again!* But who has the time for all that? Madam down there does, with her rich husband working for her and her staff doing housework—all paid for by Duncan. Not now, of course, with him dying. But she'll be all right.

I remember her from school, the dim besom. Alyssa, as she was then, wanted so much to fit in. She had a friend who wore a Tory rosette at election time. Lyssa and Angela's dad was a striking miner —*persona non grata* to that political party. She had no loyalty to her family; being popular mattered more. Her Tory pal had a rant about the miners ruining the country. She went on and on, calling them "the enemy". Angela clenched her fists, but I'd noticed that Lyssa said nothing. I feel a smirk working its way across my face at the memory of Angela shoving the ranting schoolgirl down some stairs. She'd been suspended for that. Lyssa had reported her. I bet she never regretted it for one second—Angela, I mean. But I've a feeling Lyssa would harbour no regrets either. She's more like her sister than she would ever admit.

Preston slamming the door on the way back in bumps me back to reality.

'Why is she at the flats?' I demand.

'Fuck me, her ladyship is moving in.' Preston answers in between breaths. 'It turns out, are you ready for this ...?'

I nod for him to carry on, and he sits with his hands on his knees and continues, 'You know Debbie told me her husband died abroad, and she's selling the house? I tried to squeeze out the rest of the juice from the removal men but got nowhere. So I made a quick call to Debbie to fill me in. I couldn't wait any longer. Keep it zipped 'cos Debbie said she was told not to say.'

'OK. Mum's the word.'

'She said Duncan died in Geylang. "Gay lang?" I said. "I don't know what that has got to do with it, but aye I've been gay quite a while."' He screams with laughter before pausing for effect, eyes wide.

He gets no encouragement from me. I want him to focus on the point.

Preston shrugs, 'Tough crowd. Seemingly, it is a place in Singapore. Lady Lyssa scooted off again as soon as she saw me, by the way. It transpires Duncan was married to another woman in Geylang. The wifey from abroad is holding his body hostage. The foreign wife has been left everything, so Lady Lyssa has been bombed right out of the house, on her arse.'

'Oh my God!'

'Oh, and Debbie said the woman abroad has a kid by him, after him saying he didn't want any from Lyssa,' he adds as an afterthought.

'Jesus!'

'Callum's letting her stay in the flat because she has nowhere to go for now. She has some stuff, I suppose. Angela's van and whatever.' He flicks his hand.

'What's she moving in with then? Did she keep anything?'

'Some furniture. I had a peek in one of the boxes—clothes and bags aplenty.'

'Bloody men!' I exclaim. From personal experience, I understand how enormous lies can be told and gigantic secrets kept. But this seems next level.

Preston raises an eyebrow.

'Present company excepted, Preston.' I turn to peer out of the window, but the lady in question has not returned. Instead, a green car sits where Angela's van was parked a short time ago. *Trying to avoid our gaze, no doubt.*

Preston sighs, folding his arms as he joins me at the window. 'Well, all I can say about this situation is that the sacred cows have come home to roost with a vengeance.' He fixes his stare on the removal men.

'Honestly, Preston, sometimes I have no idea what you are talking about.'

NINETEEN

LYSSA

I SIT on the edge of my Habitat sofa, propped up on my John Lewis cushions, staring around my late sister's flat. I don't care who owns what legally. I took as much as I could from the house. Moving a mansion into a flat has left me with a serious storage issue. Nothing fits in this poky little hole. Half-opened and unopened boxes are stacked against every wall in every room. Even Duncan's tools from the shed are in Angela's van. Greg and that whore can sue me if they wish.

I can't afford a cleaner, so I have no help. I should sort everything out, but I can't face doing anything. I sit in limbo, starting at the mountain of boxes. I walk over to one and open it to find the heavy antique crucifix we bought in a Tenerife market. Duncan loved old things. I take it upstairs and hang it on the bedroom wall. Then I sit on the bed to view it, rather than getting on with the job in hand.

It looks like one you would find in a kirk. I was brought up religious, and I attend Church still. When I say I was brought up religious, I don't mean kirk for a couple of hours on a Sunday. I go to normal church now, show my face for an hour and that's it. But at one point, we were evangelicals. We'd attend church all week. Sunday was the big day, of course—two services and Sunday school or bible class. Sometimes lunch was included, as it wasn't worth going home. The pastor was so animated he would bang on the pulpit and sweat. It exhausted me. I became used to counting things to pass the time.

On a Wednesday, we attended prayer meeting. We sat through hours of staring at the carpet in the back room while others prayed using words I never knew nor heard said outwith the Church. Repenting was a huge part of it. I resented repenting. The Bible doesn't say how many times you have to repent, but it seemed relentless. I hadn't time to sin before I was due to repent again.

Before Duncan died, I didn't sign up for much Christian guilt— not like my silly sister, who lapped it all up. I believed everything good that came my way was deserved. As I adjust the cross on the wall, I wonder what I did to deserve this situation. I say a prayer repenting, just in case.

I'm paying Callum a nominal rent until I sort myself out. He is busy with his course work at university and doubts he'll return to live in the town. 'Stay as long as you want,' he says. I don't want to live here at all, but it's the best offer in the circumstances. Angela's will hasn't been executed yet, so Perthshire is off the table. Callum gave me the keys to the van. He said it just needed moved, but there it is, back in its original parking space. I'd rather hide, be anonymous from the shame of it all, but instead I have to pass Rhiannon's flat downstairs every day. I risk bumping into her and Preston every time I step out the front door. How mortifying.

Before I leave, I check the window and listen in the stair to make sure they aren't around. Then I rush down to the car at breakneck speed to avoid their questions and looks. I'll be classed as the poor woman whose so-called husband died and left her penniless; the wretched widow cheated on her whole married life, the fool.

I only knew Preston as Angela's mad downstairs neighbour. She was always hanging around him. She had a boyfriend, John, but he came and went. I always told Angela she should settle down, but she was so edgy, angry all the time—even before the brain tumour.

Preston is harsh, too, with his catty remarks, which I don't like at all. It's nice to be nice, I always say. And that Rhiannon—dull as ditchwater. They think I'm stupid, but I'm not. I wasn't the one in jail, or on my own all my life—at least, not until now. A wave of depression washes over me as I remember Duncan's death all over again.

It has been two months since a Duncan-shaped hole was punched in my life. I loved him deeply, and now I grieve deeply. On the surface, I continue moving forward, being normal, keeping up appearances. Sometimes, though, unwanted tears leak out of my eyes at the oddest moments, like while I push the shopping trolley down the aisle at Waitrose. Inside, I yearn to be hysterical, to rip my clothes like the head-scarved women you see on the television who can't find their family under the rubble of a disaster zone. They'd cling to each other, wailing, while I tutted at them. Heaven forbid I could ever make such a scene.

TWENTY

RHIANNON

TWIRLING MY HAIR, I recline on the desk chair in my room, contemplating a thunderstorm and rain patterns on the windowpane. I'm procrastinating. A project gawks at me from my computer. I chuckle to myself, recalling the vision I encountered earlier today.

AS I'D STAGGERED up the bus after paying the driver, my eyes had focussed on Preston resting on the back seat, an enormous painting perched next to him. He had covered the painting with a large throw, which allowed only the subject's face to show, so she looked like a shawled woman.

'You could have taken the car,' I said, sitting down.

'Up Edinburgh? Never! Who does that? Where do you park? Nope. It's the bus all the way for me,' he babbled on, not taking a breath. 'So, the news is there have been more emails firing back and for' about the painting. This man we are going to meet sounds like he is fair looking forward to us coming to see him. He told me that working at the portrait gallery is a lovely job and all, but excitement comes few and far between.'

When we'd entered the lobby of the Scottish Portrait Gallery, an elderly lady almost careered down the steps outside, so occupied was she with Preston and his painted, scarved friend. A slim, smartly dressed man, top-to-toe in tweed with a waistcoat, yellow tie, matching hankie and fob watch, marched towards us.

'I'm the welcoming committee for this grand lady,' he announced, barely giving us a second glance as he grabbed the painting from Preston. He viewed her with glee. 'Follow me,' he added sharply, and then spun and bounded up the stairs.

We scurried behind, around the landing, and along another dark corridor, where he kicked a half-opened door leading to an office. He placed the painting against one wall as we scuttled in behind him. Gasping as if he'd forgotten to turn off the oven, he said, 'Oh! Formalities, of course! Sidney Campbell! You must be Preston.' He shook Preston's hand with vigour. 'And?'

He startled me, as I was gazing around the grandest office I had ever encountered. 'Rhiannon,' I squeaked before taking a seat.

'Have I met you before?' asked Preston with a quizzical look on his face.

'Are you a regular at the gallery? I have been here several years.'

By the time Sidney finished his statement, Preston's eyes were narrowed to slits. When the man paused to close the door behind us, Preston jumped in with, 'Nut! CC BLOOMS!'

'Ah,' Sidney giggled. 'Yes, well, I have been known to frequent Edinburgh's gay village.'

With a knowing look, Preston wandered over to the window to stare along Queen Street before returning to his seat beside me. 'It's fine and handy from here. I can almost see it from the window.'

'Indeed, indeed.' Blushing, Sidney turned his back to busy himself with the matter at hand. 'Now, let's have a look at this young lady.'

I nudged Preston and signalled to him to button his lip, as Sidney yanked off the cover.

'Eff off,' Preston mimed to me.

'She is in some state. I can't tell you anything more than you know already, based on what we see right now. Early Victorian? No, I won't say any more today. It's best we get her cleaned up.'

'Camp Sindy!' Preston almost yelled, jumping up.

I was sure my eyes were bulging at the bizarre words coming out of Preston's mouth.

'Aha! You sussed me out!' Sidney answered. As if he sensed my confusion, he explained. 'It's my drag name. Only at weekends, you know.'

Preston looked so smug, but Sidney turned once more to the painting, while I chastised Preston with my eyes.

'Leave her with me. We'll have her tarted up.' Sidney stroked his chin in contemplation. 'I've a number of connections at Historic Scotland.' He made a note on the pad on his desk. 'And the National Museum, too, might want a wee look.' He spun to face us again, his arms wide. 'Let us see if they can do some digging.'

'Thank you. We'll have a wee Google ourselves,' I answered, ushering Preston up. It was time to leave, although Preston did not appear to be taking the hint.

'See you later,' said Sidney, holding the door for us.

'Maybe at CC's,' came Preston's parting shot, as I guided him out of the door by the elbow.

'Maybe.' Sidney cleared his throat, but as the door closed, I'd seen a hint of a smile on his face.

I SMILE TO MYSELF, still staring out the window. I notice that green car again. You don't often see green cars. This time, it is pulling out of the car park. I can't make out who's driving. They better not think of parking it in the car park, or that neighbourhood watch guy on the ground floor will be on their case. I'll mention to him to keep a look out for them, in case they make a regular thing of it.

TWENTY-ONE

LYSSA

THERE'S a knock on the door. *Doesn't every story begin like that?*

I quieten my doggos and open it.

'Hiya. We thought we'd come and see how you were?' A huddle of faces crowds on the landing. I can tell by their eyes they've been drinking, probably to muster up the courage to face me.

'Want to pop down to ours?' asks Preston.

'You need company?' asks the fat one.

'No thanks,' is my immediate response. Being in this block of flats is bad enough, never mind in the murder room itself.

The fat one speaks again. 'Do you not feel like it, hen? No wonder, losing the love of your life like that.'

I stare at her, horrified.

'Okay, we'll be downstairs if you want us.' Preston rotates to push the fat one away.

'Sorry if we are a wee bit loud,' Rhiannon chips in.

'It's only us three, but ...' the fat one starts to say over her shoulder at the top step, as I smile, nod, and close the door.

I hear them giggling like stupid teenagers as they thump down the stairs, and then the sound of their flat door closing. Soon after, music starts, and I perceive the odd shriek.

I stare at my hands to convince myself I exist. Often now, by the end of the day when I am tired, I turn everything off and head up to bed, hoping tomorrow something will happen to distinguish that day from all the others.

I grip the curtain in the kitchen, ready to close it, although this flat is situated so high up that I doubt anyone could see in here. I pause, gazing out to the street. For such a busy street, it is hauntingly silent late in the evening. *There is that baseball-cap man again.* He's leaning against his car this time. He's very slight and small for a chap. It must be pick-up time for the kids at the church again. And there's the dog walker. A jogger, too. She's keen at this time of night on a Tuesday. *Tuesday.* It was a Wednesday when I got the news from Greg at his office, when the youth club emptied. I'll remember every second of that week my whole life. I peer around and the church lights are off. *Oh, who cares. I've turned into a curtain-twitcher, like that fellow on the ground floor.* I swish the curtain shut.

Tonight, at the bottom of the stairs to the bedrooms, I flick the switch to turn on the upstairs light and turn off the lower-level light, as usual. Normally—well, what has become my new normal—I'd trudge upstairs to bed. I've had three months of this new routine. Tonight, I pause.

Something inside me causes me to swap the switches. The upstairs light goes off, and the downstairs light goes on. In the flick of a switch, I move, not up to bed, but down to the kitchen. I grab some sweet wine I found in the move. I only drink dessert wine, and hardly ever. Closing the door to the flat behind me, I glide down the stairs, almost in an out-of-body dream state. By now, on a normal day, I would be sleeping. I usually need eight to ten hours religiously. But I've made a split-second, semi-conscious decision that seems like nothing.

Tonight, I'm rebelling. Rest can wait.

TWENTY-TWO

LYSSA

'OH, LYSSA! IN YOU COME!' says Preston. He bows, for no known reason. His flat appears similar but smaller, as he leads me through to where the others are on the floor, looking at CDs. They both turn to see me and exchange glances.

'Hiya!' says Rhiannon, springing up. The fat one raises herself, too. Though hardly springing, she gets to her feet surprisingly nimbly.

'Jan,' she says, as if she knows I've forgotten her name.

Jan is huge. As if in explanation, Jan adds, 'I told Rhiannon I saw this woman at Debbie's, right? Five foot and a size eight but eats as much as me at lunch—more even! She eats a massive plateful of pasta while I munch on the salad.'

'Maybe she'd fasted all week,' I suggest. I don't, out of politeness, brag that I eat what I like and never put on a pound. But I exercise. Jan is so fat, I doubt she even walks the length of herself. I wonder why people like her can't just lose weight, put a bit of effort in. But no what's-her-name (*How have I forgotten already?*) stands there like a whale, not caring.

'You want a drink, Lyssa?' Preston shouts from the kitchen area.

It is one of those poky flats where the kitchen squashes into the living area.

'I'll take a half glass of the mead I brought.'

'You want *mead*? Is this the olden times?' he quips, peering at the bottle.

'Yes.'

'Righty-ho,' he announces from behind the counter. 'Ye olde innkeeper will serve your mead.' He pours a full glass, instead of the half I demanded, and pushes it towards me.

'Can you pour some of that back into the bottle? It's too filled to the brim—hardly elegant.' I smile at the other two, who are stony-faced.

Preston flounces about on his way to the cupboards. 'Yes, my liege. Pray let me serenade you on my lute on my return.'

'When are you away this time, Jan?' starts Rhiannon, offering her a tube of Pringles.

Jan, that's her name. Jan. I'll never remember.

'A couple of weeks. Back to Marbella, and then we've a weekend in Berlin booked.'

'You're always flying off somewhere.'

'I know. We like our travels,' she replies between bites.

Preston returns with my mead decanted into two glasses, both of which he sets in front of me.

'My friend Debbie has a friend who can't get in the plane seats anymore, she grew so big,' I hear myself say. No one speaks, so I continue. 'You better watch out or you won't be jetting off anywhere at all.'

I am quite funny at times.

Jan puts down the box of Pringles. Preston picks them up and offers them around. Jan refuses. I smile. *Motivating others is another one of my strengths.*

'Jan's happily married! Seeing as we're dropping random facts,' snips Preston. Rhiannon elbows him.

'What was that?' I'm not following the conversation.

'Sorry, Lyssa,' says Rhiannon.

'I said Rhiannon and I are the single Pringles.' He almost yells, shaking the container.

'You're too fussy,' drab old Rhiannon chirps.

'I am. I dumped one once because he would kiss his whole family on the lips. I would do the air kisses or on the cheek like normal folk. One time, I went home wearing his mum's lipstick. That was the last time.'

'I dumped one because he didn't like that I used big words in conversation, Rhiannon chimes in. 'He said it made him look and feel stupid.'

'I went out with one that had long nose hairs, like curling out of his nostrils level long. I should have bought him a trimmer, but I just stopped calling him,' adds Preston.

'I had one I finished with 'cos he walked too fast,' adds Jan. They scream with laughter at this. I titter to fit in, but I don't see how she could be so fussy. *She should try walking faster herself. It might do her some good.*

'He was a foot taller, and I was always telling him, "Slow down!" I needed to totter along in heels after him. I got to the stage my bag was halfway down my arm and my coat hanging off one shoulder trying to keep up. Then I caught sight of myself in a shop window, jogging in spike heels on Edinburgh cobbles. I decided I was done with this shit. I stopped, hailed a taxi, and I never saw him again.'

'I had one too tall. My neck was sore.'

'One I went out with possessed a terrible Tweety-pie tattoo on his arse! I couldn't face it.'

'You pair should join a dating site,' suggests Jan. Preston shrieks and claps his hands.

Why is he so loud?

'Oh yes! Let's join a dating app. Try Facebook dating. It will take five minutes. It's a free one, so get yer face on it, Rhiannon.' He grabs Rhiannon's phone and parks himself beside her.

'Okay, let's see. Right, that looks a good photo. Some basic info only on there. Here we go. You are live. Let's flip through your area.'

The fat one was leaning over behind him to see. 'Nope. Nope. Nope. Stained T-shirt. Nope. Too fat. Too skinny. Boxer dog. How many of these men have a giant dog on their laps?'

'There's not much to pick between them. They're either Quasimodo or Mr. Bean,' Jan chirps.

'And how many selfies at ... what angle is that? The ten-chin angle? Every bugger knows to aim the camera down.'

'That one is standing next to a grave!' cried Rhiannon, clapping her hands.

'He should hang around it. He's not long for it himself.' Preston hands the phone to Rhiannon. 'You carry on. I'll get on the Grindr. I've signed up already.' He stops talking for a second to get his phone going. 'Mine are all ripped. I couldnae get my kit off in front of any of them, for all the judging I'd get. I could have been at the prison gym every day to kill time. I went to begin with, but even that bored me. I was in agony with my back, or it made nae difference at all.'

I gulp down the second glass of mead at the mention of prison, as they continue to scroll. I'm not sure why I'm here. They're all ignoring me anyway. I get my phone out and say, 'Do mine!'

'You want to?' asks Preston.

'Yes, but not that site. I'll pay for a decent one—aim higher.'

'Fine, if you can afford it, your ladyship,' he says, repositioning himself next to me.

'The Go Ahead dating site. The Elite Dating Agency? Exclusive Choice? Creme de la crème? The A-list dating site?'

'That one.'

'Yes, that'll be the one for you.'

I hand him my credit card and he fills in all my details. 'There you go. Take a wee scroll.'

'All grey hairs and nae hairs,' pipes up Jan, giggling. She has come over to my side of the couch. 'How about those two? Go on, like them. They look not bad.'

'Ooh, they all matched right away. Popular gal,' coos Preston.

I get a thrill. 'Should I meet them?'

'Yeah, meet them both. No problem with that,' Jan answers.

'How about this guy?' Preston nods to the screen.

I freeze. 'I know him,' I say.

'Who is he?'

'Greg Holstead. My solicitor.'

'Is he all right?'

'Yes, he's great,' I reply. Preston wavers with his drink as he reaches over and presses the button. *Like*

Within seconds, a message pops up.

Congratulations! You've matched with Greg!

TWENTY-THREE

RHIANNON

WHILE I WAIT FOR PRESTON, I rock on my desk chair, staring out at the alley where I 'saw' Kim lurking that night. I shudder, recalling the fire, almost tasting the smoke at the back of my throat. Preston bursts in, disturbing my reminisce and making me lose my balance. I gulp in air, grabbing the desk to catch myself.

'Sorry I'm late. Debbie had me hanging on for ages while I filled her in with the painting saga.'

He throws himself down on the edge of my bed, so he can stare over my shoulder at the screen. All I have in life is my work, Mother and the cats. That and the guilt. Preston and his painting are the perfect distraction.

'Patrick Thomson—so, let me put in a range of dates he might have been born in.'

'He was an adult already in 1848,' Preston suggests.

'Let's say he was born between 1768 and 1828. We'll see whether we can find someone that fits within that widest range. Then we'll narrow down our research if we need to.' I press search.

'Oh, eighty-one of them! Eighty-one Patrick Thomsons in Scotland!' He sounds disappointed.

'Come on, that's not bad for the range of ages I put in.'

'What next?'

'Let's work out if any of them were born around here, but not rule out the others yet in case he moved to the area. Here is the list.'

'No, no, no, maybe, no ...' Preston's gaze follows the list on the screen. I make notes at the side.

'Right, we have three born within a 50-mile radius. We'll start with them. We'll assume it is the one born nearest here. Any other clues?'

'His son's name is Patrick, too.'

'Let's look at this Patrick—born in 1805 ten miles down the road in Haddington. We can find out if he married. Okay, *this* Patrick Thomson married Iris in 1827. We'll come back to the other ones. Let's find out whether he had a son. We should have looked for the younger Patricks and seen whether they had a father Patrick on their birth certificate and worked backward. So, Patrick junior may have been born from about *then* to ... *then*.' I enunciate as I type the dates in, pressing search to find three possibilities.

I look up the details of the first two, but neither of their fathers was Patrick. 'This last one is born in 1834 in Musselburgh. He could fit. I'll search his certificate up.

'Yes! Father: Patrick. Occupation: baker. Mother: Iris,' Preston exclaims. 'The same guy we saw at first.'

'Yes! That must be them, the Patricks of Musselburgh. So, his dad is our Patrick then. Print the birth and marriage certificates off.'

As the clatter of the printer fires off, Preston asks, 'Is there any more information available? I'm not sure how this means we can find out who W is?'

'Just death certificates for the Patricks and Iris. I'm not sure where this leads, but we should try to glean as much information as possible.'

'Okay. Search them up, then.'

'Iris died 1834,' I say, peering at the screen. 'Oh, God! Check the date on the birth certificate for young Patrick,' I order.

Preston double checks. '1834.'

'She must have died in childbirth.'

'Oh, hell. How about the man himself, old man Patrick?'

'Died 1849—not long after writing this on the back of the picture.' He glances at the photo of the portrait on his mobile phone.

'What age was he then?' I ask.

Preston refers to the paper copy of the birth certificate. 'So ... 44. Oh, jings! That's young. Here's me calling him "old man" but he was 20 years younger than me.'

'Only twenty?' I smirk. Preston ignores my cheeky jibe. I spin to the computer again to continue my searching.

'W's turn. We know she is W.O. The wifey W needs to exist around the dates while Patrick was living,' Preston suggests.

'We can guess her birth year in a range ...' I begin

'Try find her!' He squeals. 'Winifred or Wilhelmina.'

'But we can't put her second name in. We know she's probably Winifred or Wilhelmina, but for the Scotland's People website we need a surname.'

'Oh, dead end then.' He folds his arms.

I whirl around on my desk chair and pull my cardigan on, standing at the same time.

'Where are you going?'

I halt in the doorway to answer. 'The library. They've all the old newspapers on file, I'm sure. I remember years ago it was on a thing called a microfiche. Things might have moved on from then, but they may be able to help.'

Preston stands up to follow me. 'What are we looking for?'

'His name in the newspapers, for a start, and to discover whether any prominent Wilhelminas or Winifreds were mentioned anywhere around the same time. She looks like she might have been important enough to make the papers.'

'I don't know what you're meaning, but it sounds a plan.' He rushes about, trying to find his shoes. 'And we are doing this right now?'

'Strike while the iron is burning, Preston!'

'Whit?' I hear him say, as I leave the flat.

TWENTY-FOUR

LYSSA

I'VE FELT SO powerless since I've been bereaved. I need to remind myself of my life purpose, that I can start finding things important again.

I view a profile on my phone: the architect I'm meeting for a date tomorrow. He could not be described as a poser. He looks a normal, well-built but not fat chap. He is bald, a little expressionless, and clearly inept at taking selfies. *Maybe not a bad thing for a man.* He appears very serious in his profile picture, concentrating on getting that camera button pressed. *Definitely not a seasoned pro.* I decide I like this. Duncan was clearly very seasoned at womanising, and I don't want another one like that.

And now we have a photo with his shirt off. *Thanks for that.* I spot some muscle, not a six-pack, but not a beer belly either. A good solid "dad bod". He is pale and Scottish-looking. I peruse his outdoor shots with an Alsatian dog. His bio states: 'My dog goes everywhere with me. I love walking and outdoors, castles, and stately homes.' The dog sealed the deal. I love my doggos, too.

Our messaging chats have been minimal, along the lines of, 'I like the same things you like.'

'Me too! I love food too!' So desperate are we to find a connection in common.

'I love watching TV!'

'Me too! I also love to walk!'

We have so many things in common. I've been doing the walking thing a long time now, since the age of one. Almost like we're twins, soul mates. Him, the missing half of my two-piece jigsaw. I sound sarcastic, like my sister. Still, I feel a little butterfly of excitement. *Is this how it starts—the new life? I remember this.*

When I met Duncan, I imagined it might be the beginning of my dream life. It was something all right, but all fake. My phone rings, making me drop it.

It's him.

'I was married, but it all faded away.'

I let him talk. Duncan always said men don't like women who prattle on. I know to keep quiet.

'Then I had a run of girlfriends but nothing for a while. We will go for a walk to the castle, and then lunch at the place you suggested.'

'Yes, I've booked it.'

'I've not had sex in a long time,' he blurts out.

'Me neither,' I reply, for something to say. I have an urge to hang up.

'I'd like to have sex again.'

I feel uncomfortable, but I manage to say, 'I like to get to know people first.'

'Of course.'

'See you tomorrow.'

My butterflies have subsided. A feeling of dread replaces them.

TWENTY-FIVE

LYSSA

HE IS as his picture suggested. Preston said he had a face like a spud.

I have to realise I am in the age bracket where wealthy men won't all look like Richard Gere. We are all older. He is 59. I'm 50 now. The Richard Gere ones take on 30-year-olds and younger. I have to compromise.

'This way to the castle!' he says.

I say nothing and simply take a good look at him. His face looks reddish, and flakes of skin dot his T-zone. He needs to moisturise. It might be due to an outdoors lifestyle, but I suspect it's alcohol consumption.

As if reading my mind, he asks, 'Do you take a drink?'

'Erm ... a little.'

'I don't. I'm into martial arts, so I take care of my body. And my last girlfriend was an alcoholic, so that is good.'

I seem to have passed a test. As we walk to the castle, he tries to take my hand.

'I'm not into hand holding, as such.' I swap the doggos' lead to the hand nearest him.

We arrive at the gate and ticket office.

'I'm not paying to get in,' he moans. His face reddens, and he marches away, huffing and puffing. 'Bloody ridiculous!'

'We can take a walk back,' I suggest. He strides on in front of me, his hands in his pockets. I totter behind. He comes to an abrupt halt, spins, and waits for me. When I catch up, he grabs my shoulders.

'I have a secret.'

I freeze. 'Oh.'

'I have a terminal illness.'

'Oh, God.'

'They can't fix it. They don't know how long I have. I could drop dead at any time.'

'Oh, sorry to hear that.'

'I've more to tell you. My work keeps my mind off my illness, but'—he pulls off his hat—'I had an accident on site, so I've this.' He points to a dent in his head. 'And there's this.' He takes his finger from his right hand and taps his left eye. 'My eye was gouged out in a work accident. This is a prosthesis.'

I wouldn't employ such an accident-prone architect. 'Wow, you can't tell. It is very realistic.'

His hands are back on my shoulders. 'You have lovely eyes,' he says, moving closer.

'And you have a lovely ... erm.' I pause. 'Eye.'

I release myself from his hold and walk again, gripping the lead tighter. I have no such revelations that match his. As he catches up with me, I hear him say, 'Did I tell you I'm well hung?'

'No, you didn't.' I keep my other hand in my pocket, my eyes on the path.

'Bigger than average, so you won't need to worry about that.'

'I'm not worried about that.'

'I love sex. Do you love sex?'

'I remember I did.'

'I want to have lots of sex, as I don't know how long I have. I'd like it regular. And I'm good at it. I've had no complaints.

Jesus! God in heaven above, take me now. I stop to face him. 'I'm not ready for that, and you need to stop talking about it.' I glance down, though. He isn't lying. I spot a visible bulge. I'm glad the path is busy so I don't feel I will be dragged into a bush by a one-eyed, well-hung martial arts expert with a dinted head.

'I have boundaries,' I say.

He smiles. 'And it's my job to break them down.' He laughs.

A red flag. I'd made the reservation for lunch, as I always used to for Duncan, so it felt too late to back out.

Once seated in the restaurant, he asks, 'What is your perfect day?'

I thank God for a normal conversation starter. 'A morning shopping, lunch with my girlfriends, an afternoon spa session, and then dinner and a cosy up by the fire,' I suggest.

'Me too! And then a good sex session.'

I sigh and rise to use the ladies.

'Oh, wow! Your tits are amazing.'

'Yes, they are,' I say as I walk away. I'm well aware of the breasts the doctor and I agreed on five years ago.

I sit staring at the wall in the toilet, wondering why I am here. I could be visiting that spa or going for drinks at the tennis club, instead of battling off a sex maniac with mere months to live.

'Behave,' I say on my return.

'I bet you're a good ride.' He laughs at my sigh and reaches out for my hands, which I recoil to resemble a T-rex. With luck, the food arrives to distract him.

I see him place something on the table between us. Two plastic teeth stare at me. *A partial denture adorns the table!* I struggle to swallow my food as he stuffs his face.

'I love food. I can't get enough. The more the better. I pile it high.'

We sit in silence. I am unable to speak with his second prosthetic staring at me. His food keeps him occupied. Once he comes up for air, he announces, 'Wow, we have been together almost two hours.' He looks happy. Maybe it's a record. Maybe I've lasted longer than anyone else has on a date with him.

'How do we do the bill?' he asks.

'How do we do the bill?' I repeat. Then I say and do something I've never said nor done in my life. 'I'll pay.' *I will never see you again,* I decide with the tap of my card.

We wander to Angela's stupid van in the carpark. I'd left my pooches sleeping in there while we ate. They jump up, happy to see me.

'I'd like to see you again,' he says, as I climb into the driver's seat.

'I'll message you,' I lie. I feel some guilt at being a bitch to the glass-eyed dying man, so I add, 'You could have brought your dog,' recalling his statement on his bio: "The dog goes everywhere with me."

'Oh, I gave the dog away.'

This is the end. False advertising. There is no bloody dog.

'Yeah, I gave him to the dog walker. The dog seemed to prefer him.'

Even the dog doesn't like you, I think, feeling justified as I drive away.

TWENTY-SIX

RHIANNON

'SO, it's all online now, but you may use our computers. You can use computer number two there. I'll get it up for you,' says the slender young woman at the library. She wanders over to the computer and beckons for us to sit down.

'It feels like real research now that we're in the library,' whispers Preston, sitting down.

I feel disappointed that I'm so out-of-date.

'We could go home and try to find it, now we know the link to the site,' I grumble to him. I delay taking a seat.

'I'll show you how to search, etcetera. Give you pointers on what to look for,' the lass continues. Preston does not move, so I give in and join him. The smell of the library comforts me; it's not changed since I was a child.

'What is it you are looking for?' she asks.

'Um, maybe a death notice around 1849, a Patrick Thompson.'

'Okay, you can search for names there,' she explains, pointing to the screen.

Preston types in Patrick Thomson, and a list of results pops up.

'There!' She taps the screen. 'There are a few from 1849 associated with this name.'

'Is that his death notice, or a funeral notice?' Preston asks.

'No, it's an article!' I jump in. 'Thanks. I think I have it from here.' I click on the first result from that year. She smiles and leaves us to it.

I read out the article.

'SHOCKING FIND AT LOCAL LOCH

'Yesterday morning, Mr. Patrick Thomson, an eminent and much respected Musselburgh baker, was found dead in mysterious circumstances by the seaside near Port Seton. He was in a state of undress, with many of his clothes in a pile nearby. Though it first looked like he had been swimming in the sea or had attempted to kill himself, it soon became apparent that his skull had been bashed in with what police believe to be a heavy implement. Police are seeking anyone who may have been walking along the seashore in the last two days.'

'Okay, go back to the search. Get the next one,' orders Preston. I oblige and we read quietly together.

ANNOUNCING THE FUNERAL OF THE LATE PATRICK THOMSON ON TUESDAY AT INVERESK PARISH KIRK.

Mr. Thomson was a man of unflagging energy displayed in a great variety of channels. In business, he was the owner of Thomson's bakery with his son Patrick junior. In public affairs, he served the community well, taking an important role in Inveresk Parochial Board and Inveresk Parish Council. An enthusiastic volunteer in his younger days, he assisted for a time with the Musselburgh Rifle Company. Among the youth of the town, he did good work, not only as conductor of Bible classes and the like, but as Superintendent of the Sunday School.

He was an elder of the prestigious Parish Kirk of Inveresk, a post which he held for some five years until his death. His chief hobby was as an admirer of art. Withal, he was of a kindly and courteous disposition, after the old school. He was a widower in his 44th year.

'Oh, God. He was found in mysterious circumstances. Maybe poisoned with his own loaf. Oh, speaking of loaves. I've a tribute concert to go to. A hot date,' Preston jumps up.

'What?' I question.

'You don't need to know any more than that. I like to maintain a level of mysteriousness.'

I roll my eyes.

'Usually, Preston, you'd tell me when you took a shit last. But fair enough. Leave me to it. I'll keep looking.'

'You are a gem,' he answers.

'I'll look for Wilmas, Winifreds or Wilhelminas in the papers from those dates when Patrick Thompson was alive. There may be a death notice or something about her here.'

'Jeez. Maybe I should stay. You'll be there until the cows come back.' He makes to remove his jacket, but then glances again at his watch.

'Get going, you!' I order.

He exits with, 'You're a smasher. Catch up later!'

I check out the names Wilma and Wilhelmina in the newspapers, viewing hundreds of results. Then I remember her second initial is O. There are two Wilma O's and four Wilhelmina O's, but none in the correct time period. Getting side tracked, I enjoy a delightful article about a flower-arranging competition that Wilhelmina Oswald won for her chrysanthemums in 1949, ruling that name out. So, I return to searching for Winifreds. Again, hundreds of results, so I check each one for an appropriate surname. I started too far back in time, of course. As I am accustomed to, I sort them into a logical order. With this *tick, tick* boring search, my mind wanders with thoughts that always invade my head when my mind focusses on the mundane.

My lashing out cost another human her life. Mostly, I am able to forget that event with Kim and carry on as normal. After all, I felt a weight lifted off my shoulders when I pulled the proverbial trigger and killed her—like I'd delivered justice to the bully in the end. It was irrational, but in that second, it had all made sense. Now, I realise I was hurting. Instead of asking for help, I had dialled up my bloodline's thirst for retribution. For an extended time afterwards, I continued to justify my actions. But now, somewhere in my core, I know I went too far. Kim's strangulation promoted me to a higher status of evil than any of her faults had. Sometimes now, I feel a heavy weight for stealing her life away. And Rob? I'm entirely to blame for an innocent man's incarceration, no doubt about that.

My train of thought screeches to a halt as my brain flags a pattern on the screen. A name occurs over and over in the list of search results.

Winifred Orr.

TWENTY-SEVEN

LYSSA

I PAUSE and tilt my head, imagining this scarf teamed with a jacket I already own. I could replace the one I destroyed, although I've a full box of others. I like shopping and clothes—everything else is boring. I'm not into historical monuments, crystals, and walking.

'Don't think I'm buying that for you,' states the historical monument, crystal-loving dentist I met today. He'd made a face when I said I wanted to have a look in the shop. Already, this date is not going well.

'I'm buying it myself,' I hiss, as I yank it off the rack and stomp past him to pay. This is becoming a habit. My hand is never out of my pocket these days.

I look him up and down. He is not attractive at all, but I met him as his profile mentioned he owned a holiday home in Cannes. He seemed well off, but he appears to be another skinflint. He should be grateful to spend time with me. I look young for my age. He looks grey and ancient. Sixty-two going on one hundred. He is all stooped, probably from hunching over patients' grotty mouths all day.

We are here to walk to an Abbey. I'm glad we are in the Borders, where we're not likely to meet anyone I know.

What is it with all this walking? Is that all everyone ever does? I am bored stiff. Once we are out of the shop and parked on bench, he reads out some information from a book he has.

'Dryburgh Abbey was founded by the Premonstratensian order of monks in 1152. Burned by the English in 1322, it was restored and then burned again in 1385. Rebuilt once more, it was finally destroyed in 1544. In 1786, the ruins were bought by the 11th Earl of Buchan.'

He springs up and walks in the direction of his prized old building.

'Fascinating,' I mutter, trudging behind this troll.

'My main reason for choosing this area is I'd like to see the yew tree in the grounds. I'm very much interested in yew trees.' His eyes light up and his stoop lessens with excitement.

'We have come all this way to see a tree?'

'Yes! It's a very special tree. It is claimed to have been planted by monks in 1136, but its girth does not seem to match up with this. However, historical records of growth rates show it is an extremely slow-growing yew, so despite its relatively modest girth, it could be as old as claimed.'

'And?'

'One wonders why there is such slow growth around the Abbey. And if it is as old as claimed, we must ask how it survived the devastation at Dryburgh.'

'Right,' I sigh.

'Interestingly, there is another yew here whose age can be verified by a tablet of stone. Over there.' He points. 'It was planted around 1780. It has only yielded one foot of diameter in over eighty years, confirming that yews indeed grow more slowly here for some reason.'

'So ... trees don't grow quickly around here.' I summarise. *A bit like the passing of time on this date.*

Once in the grounds, he pauses by the tree. 'Very mysterious.' He takes what looks like a pendulum from his pocket.

'What's that?'

'A crystal. They have amazing energy.'

'Oh no, that's not for me.'

'No? Are you not spiritual?'

'Definitely not. I'm Presbyterian. I don't go in for all this airy-fairy stuff. I prefer proper church.'

'I go to church.'

'Oh. yes?'

'A spiritualist church.'

'You speak to dead people?'

'Oh yes. I have a gift.'

This is the limit.

'I feel the traditional church puts a lot of guilt on people,' he continues.

'I prefer the proper church I go to.' I wander around the old tree. At least my step count will be higher today. He has a point—not so much about the church I attend now, but the evangelical one Angela and I spent our youth in when my mother experienced her rapid conversion.

Angela was very enthusiastic about it at first. She was consumed with guilt, always trying to wash her sins away, feeling rotten the whole time. I never had anything to feel guilty about. I soon returned to the normal church, the kirk, with its sense of propriety. There, the minister talked for no more than ten minutes. A couple of good old-fashioned hymns to sit through, and then home again. I don't feel guilty one bit. All good that's come to me is deserved. But I ponder why I am in this predicament now, with this ... *dentist person.*

We head to a vegetarian café of my choosing. Of course, the menu isn't good enough for him.

'I want basic fare, not all this fancy stuff.'

'Mac and cheese,' I suggest, 'isn't fancy.'

'I can make that at home,' he moans.

I don't know what he wants. Basic fare is stuff you make at home, isn't it? *Fickle little man.*

I pick a salad starter coupled with a mineral water, to watch my weight. He picks a dessert full of sugar. I wonder about his commitment to dentistry.

When the waitress arrives, he spits, 'I don't think much of your menu.'

I cringe. First an uncouth oaf, and now a rude one, too.

'Oh, it's not down to me. I don't eat anything off there either, apart from the puddings. Not my cup of tea, all that veg. Give me a good plate of mince and tatties any day,' she says, and he grins at her.

I wonder if she is single. I imagine they'd be perfectly matched, the pair of unhealthy Moaning Minnies.

Our drinks arrive, and he announces with great aplomb, 'My treat, by the way.'

At least this is a positive, although the bill won't be huge with no main courses. I am grateful that no dental appliances ornament the table—surprisingly, as I watch him pour five sachets of sugar into his coffee. *He could die soon,* I consider. *That's a positive. There is that house in Cannes.*

He is silent once the food arrives; eating, I assume. As I pick at my salad, I glance up to see him nod forwards. I watch as his head lowers down, down, down ... until he headbutts the table and jolts back up. He does not explain, simply goes back to spooning in his sticky toffee pudding.

Fabulous. My second suitor is a potentially diabetic hunchback with narcolepsy.

TWENTY-EIGHT

RHIANNON

AFTER GATHERING my papers in a neat pile on the coffee table, I begin to read out my findings. Preston perches on the edge of the sofa in anticipation. The first is a letter to the newspaper, in 1908.

'*Dear Sir,*

These words are not much to look at, but yet to me they mean a great deal. They bring back very vividly the days of my boyhood, when I went down to Miss Duff's school conducted in a small house at the very angle of Felton Green and Wonder Street. On the very spot where the Baptists are building the new hall was Mr. Whitson's grocery shop.

Everybody knew, in these days, Lady Winifred Orr, who lived in Inveresk. Few knew her as Winifred. It was just Lady Winnie who gave away her all to the poor. The likes of her have never been since, and I don't suppose will ever be again. The street used to be fairly well-lined every day with the poor and needy, waiting for her Ladyship to be coming down the

road and going to her soup kitchen, which was held in the
opening underneath the town hall, in the archway there—'

'Opposite Debbie's café,' Preston interrupts.
'Opposite Patrick Thomson's baker shop,' I correct him.
'Oh, their eyes met over a custard slice.'
I cough, and he nods at me to carry on.

'*—where all who cared to come for it got a bowl of broth and a*
roll for a halfpenny if they could afford it, and if they could not,
they got it for nothing. Well, this Mister Andrew Whitson's
shop, where the Baptist are building their hall, held the latest
stock of clogs ever, every conceivable size was there. And all
you needed to do was to get a line from her Ladyship's book
and go with it to Mr. Whitson, and you were not long in
getting a pair of beautiful, well-made clogs to keep your feet
comfortable.

Strange what the whirligig of time does. There was her
Ladyship, doing all the good she could for poor frail mortal
bodies. Now that same place is being turned into a place to be
of aid to their souls, with the Baptists planning to build a hall
there doing good works. May they be as successful as her
Ladyship was in her quest. May their work prosper and the
word of God enter into many a poor frail person's soul
through the means of the new hall is the earnest wish of yours
truly.'

'She really stuck her neck out on a limb.'
I'd learnt not to blink at such comments from Preston.
'Uh-huh. Follow me.' I lead him into my bedroom, to my I-Mac.
'What to look for now?'
'We'll need to go back to the records. We have her surname now,
so we will be able to look up so much more.'

As I type in her details to find her birth certificate, marriage and death certificate, I ask, 'Any news on your front?'

'Sidney?'

'Oh, Sidney is it? You two are on first name terms now? He is not just "the man from the portrait gallery"?'

He reddens. 'Sidney tells me the painting has gone off to the National Museum. They want to find out who she is. We might be sitting on a fortune here! Debbie says it is her money, but I'm wanting a cut. Just imagine me on *Antiques Roadshow*.'

'Money doesn't equal happiness,' I interrupt.

'Lies! Come pay day, even in the jail, I was pure buzzing!' He goes on as if he is talking to an imaginary television presenter. 'It's worth a million, you say? Oh no, I wouldn't sell her. She's far too precious to my sentimental heart.' He snorts. 'That'd be right. I'd be straight to the auctioneers!'

'She was a bit older than the baker, I see,' I interrupt again, not taking my eyes off the screen. 'Ten years.' Glancing to my desk, I hand him another paper while I busy myself scanning the information. 'Here's another document from the newspapers, while I print her certificates. It's a goodie.'

Preston reads it out as the printer fires out more paper.

'DARING BURGLARY IN MUSSELBURGH: THEFT FROM A COUNTRY HOUSE

It has transpired that a burglary of a remarkably daring character was carried out from a Musselburgh House belonging to Winifred Orr yesterday, with the loss of the sum of 30 pounds and other items. The scene of the burglary was the grand house occupied by Lady Winifred Orr in Inveresk, Musselburgh.

Indications reveal that the robbery took place about midday, whilst the family were at luncheon. After leaving the dining room, they retired upstairs to the drawing room, when, sometime

afterwards, Lady Winifred, upon entering another room,
discovered what had taken place. A wardrobe was standing open,
and when she made a closer examination, it was discovered that
an oil painting, an item of jewellery and a silk embroidered
handkerchief had been removed.

The thief got clean away. Apparently, he had entered by the front
door, and it would seem he knew something about the house and
habits of its inmates when he arranged so satisfactory an hour for
the theft. The matter has been reported to the police, who are
actively engaged in making enquiries.'

'So, now we have a cougar, a mysterious death, and a robbery!' Preston states, ticking them off on his fingers.

'And it seems the missing painting was stolen in the burglary.'

'He was in love with her, so he stole a memento of their forbidden love?' Preston suggests.

'Why forbidden, though?'

'Humble baker and posh lady? He took the painting so he could look at her whenever he wanted. Then he hid it, like a porn stash.'

I guffaw at Preston's theory. 'Are you kidding me, Preston?'

He shrugs, smirking as he peers at the photo of the painting on his phone again.

'Hi, Winifred. Now, what were you doing with the baker ten years younger, eh? Well, good for you. So what? He was a widower and you were widowed. You two might have lived happily ever after. What went on that he ended up with your picture in the attic and him dead in the water?' He looks up at me. 'My head is about burst with all this.'

'I don't know the answers.'

'Never mind that. I'm not sure I know the question.' He sighs.

'Then there's this one. She has a Wiki entry.' I produce my final document with a flourish before spinning around to face him and reading it aloud.

'*Lady Winifred Orr, known as Lady Winnie by locals, was the daughter of the Marquis of Galloway. She was widowed weeks after marrying the son of a Stirlingshire Landowner. She moved to Musselburgh, where she lived until she died in 1871. She used to walk from her home, The Grand House in Inveresk, to the soup kitchen she set up and ran from the archway at the Town Hall, giving money to those who lined the streets. Although her funeral was a private affair attended by many local dignitaries, Lords, and Knights, her cortege was followed to Inveresk by many of the poor she spent much of her life helping.*'

'Pretty much what we knew from the letter to the newspaper.'

'Apart from one thing! Come on, what is important in that document that isn't in any of the others?' I hand it to him and clap my hands in anticipation. He stares at it.

'I can't see ...'

'The Grand House.'

'Aye, a grand house. So?'

'It is not just *any* old grand house. The name of the house is THE Grand House,' I explain, not hiding my excitement.

'That rings a bell. The Grand House ... Is that not?'

With a flourish, I hand him a brochure.

'No!' he exclaims. 'Duncan and Lyssa's house!'

TWENTY-NINE

LYSSA

'HOW ARE YOU?' People ask me regularly, following Duncan's death.

'I'm okay in the circumstances,' I say, as if I learnt this phrase by heart. People want this answer, so I give it to them, although it's a lie.

'I can't even imagine,' they say.

They can. They are lying, too. They imagine it as soon as the words leave their lips. I live the grief. I don't have the luxury of imagining it. I feel like saying, 'Whether you can or can't imagine it doesn't change anything.' All they are saying is they sampled my life for a split-second and it horrified them.

Others try to minimise my loss.

'At least he didn't battle a long illness.'

'At least you still have some money.'

'At least you have somewhere to live.'

'At least you have that van.'

At least, at least, at least, at least. I add another 'at least' to my pile. It's not helpful at all to compare my situation to a worse one I could be in. Someone died. *Duncan* died. There's no bright side. This is not a glass-half-full situation.

I stop and breathe deeply when I became aware of my face contorting. All this gurning and frowning and tensing plays havoc with my wrinkles; likewise smiling too much. The money I could save on Botox if I didn't frown or laugh.

The buzzer makes me jump and sets off the doggos. Greg said he would pick me up at one, and I wasn't to worry about where we were going. *How do I dress for that?* I made the best of it, throwing on my new scarf and grabbing my Ted Baker bag on the way out.

Greg stands tall. I hadn't considered him attractive until this very second. He seems so much better than the dating site's other offerings. Plus, I have a degree of comfort with him. Those other men were unfamiliar; Greg is not.

'Hello there!' he announces, offering me his arm to walk to his car —a beautiful silver Mercedes. He opens the door for me.

'Madam.' Greg has an accent that is not placeable, as if he was born here but lived there; grew up here, but met people from there. His lilt is generic Scottish, but it's not pinable on a map. It has a nomadic Scottish twang, like Ewan MacGregor's or Lulu's.

'Where are we going?' I ask once he returns to the driver's seat.

'You'll see.' He smiles a huge grin.

I giggle like a schoolgirl. I like a man to take charge. 'Have you been on the dating site long?' I dare to ask.

'Which one?' He laughs. I pout, and he laughs again.

'A little while. I had a relationship ten years ago, as you know. I thought that was us forever. Then, I was on my own for a while. About two years ago, I was with Karina. Did you ever meet her? She lives quite near here,' he says, looking up at some flats we pass.

'Where are we going?'

'A place I know nearby.'

'What happened with her? Karina?'

'She and I were together about a year. I moved in for a few months, and then she dumped me inexplicably. Two years have passed since.'

'Why?'

'As I said, inexplicable. I put a lot of investment into that relationship. It floored me for a while. Do you understand?'

'Yes.'

'Yes, of course you do.'

We don't speak for another five minutes.

'It took me quite a while to get over that,' he mutters, tapping the steering wheel. Then he announces, 'Here we are!'

Again, he opens the car door for me, and once more takes my arm. We find a cosy corner in the country restaurant, our knees almost touching. This time, it feels like a date.

'Have you been on the dating site long?' he asks.

'Which one?' I ask. I am quite cheeky at times.

He laughs. 'Great stuff, Lyssa!'

'I had two dates, both disastrous.'

'I've had a few disasters. I met one—she was married, and her husband showed up. Then another could not speak a word of English. She'd been using Google translate to chat. Then, I had one nightmare two-week fling, pre-Karina, about five years ago.'

'A nightmare?'

'She stalked me. Wouldn't leave me alone for years! She was totally obsessed. Let my tyres down once when I met someone else ages later.'

I feel a pang of jealousy.

'She seemed fine, an attractive woman, a little older than me. Then it became clear she was plain weird, into crystals and nonsense. She seemed normal until all this hippy stuff came out.'

'Oh, I met one liked crystals, too! And speaking to dead people.'

'She loved all that. She said her dead granny told her we were destined to be together; hence, she wouldn't leave me alone.'

'She sounds crazy.'

'She was. She'd meet my friends and tell them we were still together years later, although we never were. It was a fling, nothing more. She was into Tarot and all sorts.'

Greg pays for everything and drives me home. His driving leaves a lot to be desired. At one point, he even goes through a red light, but somehow it thrills me. At the door, I find myself saying yes when he asks for a kiss. He pulls me towards him and kisses me fully. I am taken aback at its ferocity. I almost forget to breathe.

'I'll head off. I have some work to catch up with in the office.' I glance over at his office, across the road from these flats. A sinking feeling reminds me of my recent visit there to find out about Duncan's will. I consider him gallant to not ask to come up. He showed respect. But by the time I get to the door of my flat, I'm worried that maybe he didn't fancy me.

No, that kiss told a story. Within half an hour, my phone pings.

Thanks for a lovely lunch date.
You are wonderful company x

I blush. I take a couple of hours to stretch. I'm using the Pilates DVD at 'home' now to save money on classes. Afterwards, I take a relaxing bath, put on my nightdress and read a magazine. My phone pings again.

Hey there. Do you want a visitor?
I've finished at work now x

Hmmn, is this a booty call?

I'm in bed already. Goodnight.

I'm not in bed, but I jump under the covers so it's not a complete lie. I should take offence that he believes it's acceptable to make a move this soon, but I'm flattered. I giggle as I put my phone on silent and turn off the light.

My phone vibrates within seconds. I'd usually ignore it, to get my beauty sleep, but my curiosity gets the better of me. *Is it him?* No.

It's a friend request on Facebook from a woman. Louise Lacey. I can't place the name. I check her profile. She's a local woman. We have no mutual friends, which is unusual as I've lived here all my life. She attended Elgin School. Elgin? Isn't that near Inverness? She must be from the north of Scotland and have moved here.

I check her photo. She's attractive, perhaps in her late thirties or early forties. She somehow looks familiar. I flip through her profile shots. A poodle on the end of a leash with her foot showing, and another poodle shot on her lap. Her interests include dogs, walking (another one!) the Conan Doyle Centre Edinburgh, Tarot readings. Her profile is closed, so I cannot see any of her posts. Her cover photo is a stock photo of a pair of hands holding a large crystal. I sit upright in bed.

A crystal!

THIRTY

RHIANNON

'HIYA!' screams Preston, bounding through the flat door and waving an envelope.

'I have to catch the bus.' I stop him in his tracks.

'Where you going? Registers house?' He fingers the envelope and his face falls, his head dropping.

'No. I couldn't make an appointment for a while.'

'So, where?' He pouts, his eyes still on the letter. I watch him rip it open.

'I told you this morning, a work course.'

'Sit down, this will take minutes.' He pulls the letter out of the envelope.

Intrigued, I ask, 'What have you got there?' He waves it again, grinning, and spins me around, guiding me into the living room to park me in the armchair.

'A letter from Sidney at the Scottish National Portrait Gallery. I'll read it. No, no, you read it, Rhiannon. You read it,' he demands, holding it out. He reclines on the couch to listen.

'Let me get comfy. Go!'

'Okay,' I reply, standing up. I straighten my back and breathe in, pausing for tension.

'Dear Mr. Field,
I am writing regarding the found painting in Musselburgh
High Street. I can confirm I have reviewed said oil painting on
canvas brought to the attention of The Scottish National
Portrait Gallery. It would appear to have a similar style to
other Scottish portrait painters, such as Alan Ramsay and
Henry Raeburn, though it is not thought to be from either of
these artists, whose work is well recognised.'

'How does he know? Maybe Raeburn did it on the sly,' Preston interjects, sitting up.
'He is an expert.'
'Ugh! Nae millions for me!' Preston exclaims, throwing himself back to horizontal.
I carry on reading.

'Among those well-known of the story, suggestions abound
about the identity of the lady.'

'That'll be me.' Preston interrupts and props himself up on his elbows again.
'Oh yes. You are always abounding with suggestions.' I laugh.
'My suggestions are always bountiful,' he replies, to my accompanying snort.

'In the early nineteenth century, to which this painting is
assumed to be dated, the lady's sombre dress, presumably
Georgian or early Victorian, points to her being a widow of
this era.'

'No shit, Sherlock!' Preston leans forward for more.

'At this time, it was mainly the aristocracy who could afford to have their portrait painted.'

'I said that. I said that to Debbie!'

'The house in which the painting was found does not seem grand enough, although at that time, several houses in and around Musselburgh were of high quality. There were several large house and estates in the surrounding area, the closest being Pinkie House, although Inveresk Village would be the most obvious place.'

'I guessed that, too. And we know the actual address!'

'She may well have been a daughter of one of those families, perhaps Catholic, as a cross hangs on the wall behind her. The brooch at the neck of her blouse seems too large for a mourning brooch, thus is more likely a cameo—a popular piece of informal jewellery at the time. She appears to be wearing a black embroidered net shawl, which sits over her head and falls around her shoulders. Her long hair is fixed in plaits to the sides of her head. A long chain hangs around her neck. What hangs from the chain is not visible, due the erosion of the paintwork. There is a possibility she is the daughter of a prominent family, who had fallen from grace and was living in reduced circumstance, perhaps in the house. However, no maps at that time mention any such woman. A Mr. Thomson was living there behind the bakery at the time, presumably the baker. However, a woman would scarcely be mentioned unless she solely owned the property. Recourse to further census failed to shed more light on the subject. In any event, there

seems no way of positively identifying which incumbent of the property secreted the picture or why. The letters P.T., on the back of the painting implicate the aforesaid Mr. Thomson further, and the initials W.O. are mentioned, pointing to being those of the lady in the picture.'

'You never filled him in on our findings?'
'Not yet. I might suggest a meeting to discuss this.' He smirks.

'The inscription was written in 1848, dating the painting earlier and confirming it is Victorian era. The restored picture, which is loosely reminiscent of Da Vinci's Mona Lisa, *has an indefinable presence, although obviously not by that artist, the subject has an enigmatic smile.'*

I let up and glance up from the document, but this time, Preston doesn't interrupt.

'Was she smiling to tempt a love, or was she indeed a widow smiling to hide a sad and lonely heart? Unless some member of the public sheds further light, the lady's story may remain a permanent mystery. One thing is certain: someone cared enough about her not to destroy her image but to hide it away, perhaps in the hope she would be rediscovered one day, cherished and admired again by her new owner. Whoever she is, and whatever she had done in her life, she has found a new status as the mystery lady of Musselburgh.

Kind regards,
Sidney Campbell.'

'Blah blah blah, and his number.'
'Pretty much what we knew already, but he put it posher.'

'Indeed. It was beautifully put. Now, I gotta go!' I head out the door.

'He has a lovely way with words, the snobby old bugger. I think I'll give him a wee call,' I hear Preston add, his voice wafting down the stairwell as the flat door closes.

THIRTY-ONE

LYSSA

MY SECOND DATE with Greg has been three weeks in the waiting, due to his work commitments, but I feel excited and then a bit of a pang. Jan maintains I have survivor guilt—that feeling of being happy, laughing and then feeling guilty, as if I should be unhappy or sad. I remind myself: *You are what you think.*

I imagine myself happy, as I was before. Then a crushing guilt feeling takes over. *What kind of monster feels happy in this situation?* I make a decision. *I will feel happy. I will enjoy a day at the races with Greg, and then dinner.*

My mind wanders to the friend request from Louise Lacey. I accepted it out of pure nosiness, concluding she must be his stalker lady, but nothing came of it. Maybe I was being paranoid. Lots of people like crystals, after all. On impulse, I Google the Arthur Conan Doyle Centre, one of her interests. I'm disappointed to find it is a spiritualist church in Edinburgh. This adds up, as Greg said she dabbled in spiritualism. *Maybe she knows the bent-over dentist I dated.*

The buzzer and the doggos' barking signal me to stop this nonsensical thinking and descend the stairs. I'm about to enjoy another delightful day with Greg. I'm glad that, at last, I have a chance to dress up and have a day out.

Greg is dressed very smartly and is charming, as always. 'You look wonderful,' he gushes, taking my arm.

I make to walk to the racecourse, but he stops me. 'Your carriage.' He indicates his car.

'Oh, we don't need the car today. It's not far.'

'I insist,' he replies, guiding me to the open passenger door. 'It's a while since I've blessed a racecourse with my presence.'

'Oh, yes?'

'I like the spectacle of it all, and the horses, but to be honest, I hate gambling.'

'You won't have a flutter?'

'No, but you go ahead. I don't hold with it. My grandfather was what would be described today as a gambling addict.'

'Really?'

'Yes. He lost it all. Sold what should have been the family home when I was ten. It's made me rather risk averse, to tell you the truth'

AFTER A FEW WINS and some Prosecco, I freshen up in the ladies. Greg has smudged my lipstick several times already. It's inappropriate, with people watching, but I giggle to myself as I touch up my make-up. On my return, he watches me walk over to him.

'Ah, Lyssa,' he beams, and I smile. 'You wouldn't believe this, but something has come up.'

'Oh?'

'I have some work to attend to. Would it be okay if I went to the office for a couple of hours? Say we head back after the last race, about 3:45pm?'

'But dinner?' *Is this the brush off? Why?*

'Oh, we can still meet for dinner if it suits you. It won't take too

long. My client Fraser McIntyre, you'll know him from the rotary?'
He fumbles in his pocket for his phone.

'Yes, yes, Fraser.'

'He has messaged, and it's urgent. I could drop you at the flat.'

I shrug, somewhat bewildered.

'You might want to change. Have a little rest while I pop in the
office and sort this out.'

Is it female intuition, making me feel like something is off?

'I'll call the restaurant—let them know we'll be a little later,' he
suggests.

What is this feeling? I'm ... perturbed—that's the word. *How
irregular, to disappear in the middle of a date.*

'Say 7:30? That gives me a good few hours to sort everything out
and deliver it to him.'

Duncan was a businessman, too, I reason. *He often rushed off to
meetings—Oh!*

'Then you can have me all to yourself,' Greg adds.

He must notice my pout.

'You have to understand. I have a business to run.'

It feels like a telling-off, but then he pulls me in and kisses me in
front of everyone. A woman I know walks by, tutting. I gasp.

'Is that all right, beautiful?' he whispers, an inch from my face.

I melt. 'Oh, that's fine.' There is a more suitable dress I can wear
to dinner. It's so difficult to dress for day to night.

'How lovely you are, so accommodating.' His phone vibrates.
'Och! Don't tell me,' he moans, peering at his messages. 'See!' He
shows me his phone message, displaying the name Fraser McIntyre,
and the message.

> **I simply must have the doc today, Greg.
> If you could be a good chap and
> send that over. Thanks.**

'I owe him a favour, you see. Where are my car keys now?' He flusters. He presses the 'back' button absentmindedly to close Fraser's message. A list of messages appears. Fraser's name is there, but another name also jumps out at me.

Louise Lacey: Answer me n—
Fraser McIntyre: I simply m—

The woman who added me on Facebook three weeks ago appears to be the last person to message him. The one I thought may be the lady Greg said he couldn't get rid of.

Why is she messaging him now?
And why is his stalker not blocked on his phone?

THIRTY-TWO

LYSSA

HE DROPS ME OFF, seemingly not noticing my silence.

Men like women who don't talk too much, I remember. *All will be well.*

He kisses me in a way that leaves me with no doubt of his intentions.

As I change for dinner, I don't know what to think. *Has my experience with Duncan made me into a suspicious woman?* I check myself out. I look beautiful in pale blue. *Why would he not want me?* I give myself a shake. I've never had any reason to feel insecure, and I'm not starting now.

AT DINNER, Greg kisses me in front of everyone. He is proud to be seen with me. He flirts outrageously, his hands on my knee or holding mine.

I toy with my food. No man wants a woman wolfing food down like a pig. My mind turns to where this is leading. *Should I let him stay tonight?* Callum is due tomorrow for a stopover before heading to the airport. It could be awkward, but I don't want to put Greg off.

'It might be tricky tomorrow morning if you …'

'Tomorrow morning?' He blusters. 'Oh, oh! You don't think I'm expecting to stay over?'

'I-I thought maybe you might be … but my nephew …'

He shakes his head, and I redden.

'No, no. I wasn't expecting that at all.' He laughs, as if I've proposed something ridiculous.

I feel myself cringing. 'I'll pop to the ladies.'

'Of course.'

I stare into the mirror, my face flushed. I've embarrassed myself. I got the wrong end of the stick. *He'll believe I'm a hussy!* Yet two weeks ago, he booty called me? *What does he mean, making me feel stupid for believing he might want to stay the night?*

I keep doing this. What is this feeling? When I exit the toilets, I see a back door. *I could leave now, run away.*

I take a moment to pull myself together. All this overthinking is not feminine. I brush it off. Thankfully, Greg seems not to have taken offence and is delightful company for the rest of the evening.

WHEN WE'RE BACK at mine, I let him into the flat. I've made up my mind. I'll sleep with him tonight, Callum or no Callum. Greg kisses me passionately as soon as we are in the flat. As I lead him upstairs to the bedroom, his phone rings.

I stop on the landing. 'Who is that calling?' I ask, with my hand on his chest.

'No one,' he replies with a smile. He leans into me.

'No one?' I stop him with one palm up. 'It's very late.'

'Midnight,' he says, glancing at his watch.

I feel that pang of insecurity in me again. 'I'm exhausted with all the excitement. I'm overwhelmed, so not tonight,' I hear myself saying.

'Playing hard to get, eh?' He laughs, but then immediately adds, 'No, no, I'm joking. Of course, of course. It's all a bit much too soon for you, my angel.' He kisses me on the forehead.

After one more delicious kiss at the door, he leaves. I climb the stairs to my bedroom, still wondering whether I should have let him stay. Someday there must be a first time with Greg. My phone pings as soon as I lie down. I expect it's a goodnight message. It is a message, but not from Greg.

Louise: Hey are you done?

Louise Lacey! I sit upright and don't answer for a minute. Curious, I reply.

Yes

Louise: Gregsy, you are late this time, you dog. I waited outside Lyssa's for ages. Get in my bed in 5 minutes. It's still warm from this afternoon lol xx

I think to reply, but in a flash, all her messages to me are unsent.

THIRTY-THREE

RHIANNON

THERE'S NEVER A TIME, even when I appear happy, that I've forgotten the deed. After the event came the shock—the horror-filled memories and dreams of what had happened. Thoughts of overdue karma overwhelm me. I've got away with murder. I didn't attend any counselling, and none was offered. Of course, the authorities were not aware of my direct involvement, but they'd be aware I was traumatised by the event. I've never spoken with anyone about Kim's murder. I feel guilt carrying on with my normal life while her life has been snuffed out at my will! I'll never escape it. I often jerk awake with the sensation of hurtling out of control; my dreams lead towards the scene of the crime, as if transported there. I still hike, but I never walk along the lagoons in case I see it all again.

Preston flies into the kitchen and opens the fridge door, interrupting my thoughts. 'Hiya. Never anything to eat in this house.' He pivots to face me. 'Have you found her will yet?'

'No. I have to talk to the national register folk about that.'

'When you going?'

'I've made an appointment. I told you.'

'When is it?'

'A good three weeks away.'

'No way! How many folks are investigating like us?'

'It's the fashion to look up your ancestors. It became a lockdown craze. My pal Ian has talked me through it all.'

'So you'll find her will.'

'If she left one. She was rich and lived in a decent home, so let's hope so. But it will be handwritten. Ordering online is possible, but it takes a similar time. Ian works there, and he's good at Scots language. If I go up, he'll interpret it and type it out for me, so we're able to understand it.'

The buzzer interrupts us.

'Jesus! Can the volume of that thing not be turned down? I nearly had a stroke!' Preston moans, as he pads along the hall to let it whomever it is in, without even checking.

'Who is it?' I yell from the living area.

'Didnae ask. I'm playing intercom roulette. Did you order anything?' he shouts, leaning against the doorframe.

Jan arrives, waving a newspaper. 'Have you seen this?' she asks. 'It's got your article in it, Preston!'

'Ooh, my article!'

'What article?' I chip in.

'A journalist from the paper visited the café. She came to speak to Debbie after Debs put something about finding the painting up on Facebook. And voila!' Jan flips open the paper to the appropriate page on the breakfast bar. We peer at a half-page photo of the portrait and a smaller, inset image of Preston and Debbie holding it. Preston grabs it, hands it to me, then runs around to recline on the sofa.

'Read it, Rhiannon. Read it!'

'Okay. Ahem.' I straighten up and shake out the local newspaper.

'LADY HENRIETTA REMAINS A MYSTERY!

'Forget the Mona Lisa, *Musselburgh now has its own mystery lady to rival Leonardo da Vinci's world-famous beauty. Residents in the*

town are being asked for their help in identifying the subject of a 19th-Century painting that lay hidden to the world for decades.

'Discovered in an outbuilding by Preston Field and Debbie Kerr (the owner of Debbie's café in Musselburgh High Street), the mysterious lady with the barely detectable smile has so far left experts baffled.

'Preston and Debbie stumbled upon the painting when they decided to convert a back room of the café. The room was once a house belonging to the old baker and may have been used as a henhouse, hence why we have nicknamed her Henrietta! With the help of Musselburgh News, they hope to solve the riddle of the mystery lady and wonder if anyone in the local area recognises the face.

'It all begs the question: Who is she, and why was she hidden away?

'"She must have been of some importance to have her face painted in oils," suggests Preston. "The rafters had been cut out so that the painting could be placed into the ceiling. It was damp, and it had been eaten by mice. It must have been there for donkey's years, and we never ever knew about it."

'The Scottish Portrait gallery in Edinburgh dated the picture to the 1800s from the way the subject was dressed and the type of materials used. Not to mention the date on an inscription on the back—1848, a bit of a giveaway! As for Henrietta's identity, all they could suggest was that she was perhaps a young widow. We in the newsroom believe that would explain her plain black dress. Initials on the back were P.T. and W.O.—another clue in the puzzle? We think so! But why was she up in there in the ceiling? Had she been stolen and hidden away?

Musselburgh Museum could be the next call. Anyone who can help solve the mystery or provide information is asked to contact Preston at …

'And then your number.' I sit down again.

'Should you have put your number out there, Preston? You might get all sorts of nutters calling you,' Jan suggests, biting her lip.

'Ah, it'll be grand. I'm a nutter-magnet any roads. You know that famous saying—'

We pause, hanging on his impending words.

'Birds of a feather flock like a duck to water.'

THIRTY-FOUR

LYSSA

Morning gorgeous. How are you? xx

I STARE at the text from Greg. It has been three hours, and I have not yet answered. I am exhausted. I read in my magazine that sleep is often affected by stress. Insomnia is common, but not for me. Stress made me sleep more last night than on a normal night.

Once I'd calmed down about those messages from Louise Lacey, with my doggos for company, I'd dropped off and slept eleven hours. My sleep had been full of dreams, however.

I'm all over the place. I have no head space to deal with everything else that needs my attention, like the fact that maybe I should get a job. I'm behaving illogically. Emotionally, even. In one moment, I think *I'm bigger than this* and I feel powerful. In the next, I am lost to victimhood, feeling sorry for myself, coming close to tears. My brain runs wild with thoughts.

What will people think?

This is my fault for dating so soon.

I hate him for doing this to me.

I hate her for doing this to me.

I'm acting like someone else entirely, like my personality is changing.

I peer out the kitchen window, looking for Greg's car. Of course, it's long gone. I hope to catch a glimpse of him in his office. If I lean to the left, I can spot his office from across the road, but I see nothing of note. He'd hardly be standing in the shop window.

Oh God, I nearly slept with him, too. I am glad I didn't. I did well not to.

My mind keeps firing questions.

How long would she have waited outside?

Why was she there?

How did she know he was at mine?

And who the hell is she?

I don't know what is happening to me. I've never thought this much my whole life. I can't even concentrate enough to sit down and read one of my 'books'.

What is the point in reading about interior design when I've no house to design?

Why can't I stop?

I Google her name and find nothing. No trace apart from her Facebook profile. What the hell? It seems like she doesn't exist. Greg did say it was 'no one' calling him.

My phone pings, and I jump. The architect. Ugh! I ignore it. It pings again. The spiritualist, crystal-loving dentist. I open that one up.

Hi Lyssa, I was wondering if you'd like a chat.

I press the call button.

'Hi! I wasn't expecting so quick a response. How lovely.' He sounds happy.

'Hi. I need to pick your brains. Something has happened which has distressed me.'

'OK, I'm sure I can help. We could meet for coffee, I know a lovely church, we could—'

'No, not a date.'

'Oh!' His voice drops. 'Then what?'

'I need to ask you a strange question.'

'Go on.'

'Do you know a lady called Louise Lacey?'

'I don't think so.'

'She likes crystals. She goes to the Conan Doyle Centre.'

'Oh, right. She may be part of the spiritualist community. I could ask around. The name sounds familiar. What does she look like?'

'Slim. Brown hair. I have a photo of a woman of about forty years old, but Greg said she's older than him.'

'Who is Greg?'

'The man I'm dating.' I don't want to call him anything more than that.

'Sorry, what is this all about?' He bites.

I sigh and fill him in on an edited version of the events and her messages.

'And you say he was in your flat?'

'Um, yes.'

He pauses. 'Maybe you should be more discerning about who you have in your flat.'

'Oh!' I muster. 'He told me she was an ex. I believed him. He said she was a stalker. She was outside my flat at midnight, though, so that fits. Oh, I don't know what to think.'

'I do. Her man is cheating on her with some floozie.'

'I'm not a floozie!'

'Yes, I'm afraid you are. I'll ask around the community. See if she needs checked on.'

I hang up. *Stupid dentist!*

I type out a message to Greg. It's 1pm, and I assume he takes a lunch break.

I need a chat. I will be in Debbie's café in 20 minutes.

I DELETE IT. Then type it again. But I leave it and don't send it. I pull on my boots and then press 'send'. I march past his office and down the street to Debbie's café. If he answers in the time it takes me to sit there and drink a coffee, I shall speak to him again. If not, I will abandon this whole affair.

THIRTY-FIVE

LYSSA

I TAKE a seat in Debbie's café and remove my pashmina. Greg's time is running out. As I wait to be served, my phone lights up.

> **I can meet you now x**

I'm here at Debbie's. I want to talk.
I've heard from Louise. She messaged me.

> **Oh God, block her! I'll be there in 5 x**

Talking only. No funny business

> **It must be on your mind ;-) x**

He's a nerve, joking about that, knowing what I know.

'We don't usually see you in here. What're you up to today?' I hear a voice ask. It's Debbie herself.

'Meeting someone.'

'Oh, who?'

'Greg Holstead.'

'Oh, Greg! Yeah, I know Greg.' She laughs and rolls her eyes.

'He's my solicitor,' I say, dry as the desert. That wipes the smile off her face. *What is she giggling at anyway?*

'Oh, right. Oh, yes. I see. How are you?'

'I'm okay.' No one knows what to say in these circumstances, but I know what they want to hear.

'I'm glad to hear it, darling. Preston will take your order.'

'Two Americanos,' I bark.

'Ah, I don't take the orders. Preston...' She stops in her tracks, as my glare freezes her.

'I'll just get that for you,' she mutters, scuttling off.

I peer out the window at the passers-by and list them. People my age with walking aids. Young mothers with buggies laden with shopping. Solitary men walking with their hands stuffed in their pockets. Mum would say, 'Why aren't they at work?' whenever ever she saw a man in the daytime. And a slim dark figure sitting in a car, waiting. Baseball-cap man is waiting here now, too. There's no church pick-up in this area. *What does he do all day?*

Greg flies in and parks himself opposite. He reaches his hand to mine, but I pull it back. I stare at him, poker-faced.

'So?'

'So, Louise messaged me.'

'And?'

'She said you saw her yesterday'

'I did,' he states without a blink and reaches for the sugar sachet.

'What?' I reel back in my chair, shocked there is no denial.

'I did, as she said she'd been taken ill.'

'What?'

'I thought I was being kind. I did have to work, too, but I didn't mention I was checking in on her. I knew it would result in so many questions.'

'She said she was waiting outside last night.'

'Stalker behaviour, no? I did tell you.' He stirs his coffee slowly.

'She implied you did more than check in on her.'

He rocks back in his chair. 'Lies. She is pitiful. My problem is, I am too nice. I keep getting hauled back by her. I simply give her the time of day or treat her the way I would any person, and she blows it up into *We are a couple*.' He looks tired and truly exasperated.

'The messages looked like they were for you, though. As if she'd accidently sent them to me. She deleted them pretty speedily.'

'Oh, she's good all right. Classic Louise. If you quizzed her, she'd make out she had had too many drinks and messaged you by mistake. Whoopsie.'

'Maybe that's what happened.'

'Except she doesn't drink. She's a stalwart member of the local A.A. Goes to a meeting every Monday night. She'll have done it on purpose, making out we are still on,' he insists. 'Karina tired of her drama. It drove her to paranoia, as she often believed Louise to an extent. She devastated my relationship with Karina two years ago.'

'Where is Karina?' I glance out the window. Baseball-cap man is still there. 'You mentioned something about her living around here'

'Still local, I guess. She lived over the bridge. She may have moved. I don't hear from her now.'

There's a tap on the window. Fraser McIntyre stands there, hands on hips. He nods to me, and I nod back. Greg's demeanour changes as he waves at Fraser.

He rises. 'Ah, two seconds. Fraser demands my attention, yet again.'

He nips out, and I watch his back through the window. They seem to be arguing. Greg really is a fine figure of a man. I look away and spot his phone facedown on the table. I almost tap on the glass to let him know I have it, but then I stop myself. Reaching out, I slowly pull it towards me. I tug my pashmina over my arm to cover my actions. With one eye on Greg, I open it up. No lock on it, foolishly. I press to see a list of texts and take a mental photograph of it. Then I replace the phone when I see Preston approaching with our coffees. I still have the image of the phone screen in my mind, as

I smile and say in a voice more high-pitched than I expected, 'Thank you.'

> **Lyssa: It must be o—**
> **Karina: I don't kno—**
> **Robyn Khafoor: XXXX**
> **Louise Lacey: Answer me n—**
> **Fraser McIntyre: I simply m—**

THIRTY-SIX

LYSSA

'YES, the date with Greg was wonderful,' I explain, giving the gang the run down. 'The negatives? He could have three women on the go.'

'Three!' Rhiannon exclaims.

Rhiannon, the fat one, and Preston stare back at me. I swirl my fifth glass of mead in the murder flat. I never used to drink this much.

Preston summarises. 'Right, we have number one: Louise the maybe stalker. Number two: the ex, Karina. And number three: Robyn, the last one.'

'Hells bells,' the fat one mutters.

Preston stands up. 'Rhiannon, get on the Facebook. Search madam Louise's FB profile. Dinnae you worry, hen. Stalky Stalkerson over there is on the case.'

'Her profile looks fake. Look at her photo. It looks like it was taken in a studio,' the fat one suggests, peering over Rhiannon's shoulder.

'She messaged me. She is real.' I insist.

'Anyone recognise her?' Preston asks. They all shake their heads.

'It says here she went to Elgin School,' Rhiannon adds.

'Where's that?' asks the fat one.

'Elgin is up north, isn't it?' I suggest.

'Give me a minute.' Rhiannon does some Googling. 'Elgin School ... Louise Lacey,' she says slowly.

'Are you okay for a drink, hen?' Preston asks.

I hold out my glass as an answer.

'What the hell? She's a Kiwi!' Rhiannon exclaims.

'A Kiwi? What you mean a Kiwi?' Preston squeals.

'Like the fruit?' Jan quizzes.

'I once went out with a guy thought he was an orange,' says Preston from the kitchen, where he's pouring my drink. No one comments. 'He fell to pieces.'

'Uh-huh, very funny,' says Rhiannon drily.

I don't understand what Preston is talking about most of the time. Something about him unnerves me. As he hands me my drink, he continues, 'Explanation, Rhiannon.'

'I've found a Facebook post for Elgin School in New Zealand. It reads, "Hey, I've made a list of the class of '78 for the reunion. I've put in the whereabouts of everyone and a little list of those I can't find." Under the list of folks this person can't find is the name Louise Lacey.'

'So, they can't find her either.' Jan sticks her lower lip out. She needs to watch out or her expressions will wrinkle her face right up.

'Class of what now? 1978. So, say she was sixteen to eighteen when she left? What does that make her?' asks Rhiannon, still staring at her screen.

'In her sixties.'

'Bloody hell! Old enough to know better. But her photo ...?'

'An old one. A classic ploy. I'd do the same.' Preston brushes it off.

'Greg did say she was older,' I manage to squeak. I feel less intimidated by a pensioner.

'Let's move on to number two: Karina. This one sounds like she was the love of his life.'

I shift in my chair at that comment. 'Any second name? Lives around here, by the bridge. We're able to see the river from here, and Greg's office is across the road. He doesn't go far, does he? Anyone else know a Karina?'

'Nope.'

'I don't know her. But there's her profile. The top local Karina that comes up with a liked profile picture by Greg Holstead himself.'

'Let me see.' I grab the iPad off Rhiannon. She's a slim, blonde woman of about fifty-five. She's not petite like me, rather she is tall, a bit horsey-faced and wrinkly with straggly hair. I feel happier, seeing her averageness. I hand the iPad back to Rhiannon and lean into the sofa.

'You take a bonny picture, Lyssa. That Karina, she has too long a neck. All those folks with swan-like necks going about sicken me, bloody peering about like meerkats. I call them the giraffe people,' Jan says. 'I don't trust them. I'm not in the neck club myself. I used to have a bit of neck, but now it's all just chin. A couple of chins, and then a bosom. No, not for me, those kind of people.'

'That's a lot of animal references, Jan. Have you ever wondered what animal you are?' Preston asks, following with, 'I am a wolf.'

'Mmm, a cat,' adds Rhiannon.

'I like cats,' I say, just to join in, 'but I like dogs better.'

'I like elephants. Most folk would say that's because I'm fat and lumbering, but I like them for their loyalty. They go to other elephants' funerals.'

I don't know why the fat one has perched herself next to me while I update them on my disastrous dating, but I remember she was nice about my photogenic qualities.

'Have you lost weight, Jan?' I venture.

'Yes.'

'I can tell.'

Jan gives me a wry smile and shakes her head. 'I've gone from 18 stone to 17 stone in six months, Lyssa. I'm no' exactly slimmer of the year.'

'Number three! Moving on, people. We have a full name—Robyn Khafoor. Rhiannon, get on it.'

'I've her Facebook. I could carry out different searches on all of them, try to find them on the electoral register, land registry, court records and discover more?'

'Let's get the basics before you go full on Columbo. Let's take a look at Robyn.'

I look over her shoulder to see a dark-skinned woman, very different from the other two.

'This one is younger. She's thirty-four,' states Rhiannon.

I flinch, but Jan leans in and screws up her face as she peers at the photograph.

'Jings! I've a big behind, but that lassie looks like she could carry a bread board on her arse. She's not a patch on you, Lyssa,' Jan says, rubbing my arm. It is reassuring. I decide everyone needs a pal like Jan.

'You see, you need to make a stand here, Lyssa. Sounds like you could do much better than this womanising Greg fellow,' Preston announces.

'But what if it's all harmless? I like to put kisses on messages, like Robyn,' says Jan.

'He lied! He said he hadn't heard from Karina,' Preston argues.

'You should mention it to him. Stand up for yourself. Get it all straightened out.'

'Oh yeah, Jan, 'cos you are so good at standing up for yourself.' Preston guffaws.

Jan just giggles. 'Oh, I know. I say I'll say this and that, and I imagine it all in my head. But then when I see them, I say nothing.'

'I know what animal you are! You are a jellyfish,' Preston exclaims.

'Jellyfish aren't nice.'

'Quite beautiful when you see them in the water. Less so washed up on the beach,' Rhiannon pipes up.

'Why am I a jellyfish?'

'This is you.' Preston lies on the floor, flapping around.

I hide behind my drink, recoiling at the whole scene.

'I'll show you. I'll show you. Oh no, I can't. I'm a jellyfish. I've no backbone.'

Jan joins him on the floor.

What is she doing?

'I'll show you! You run right over me, like the doormat I am.'

Rhiannon pulls me to the ground, so we are all lying on the ground on our backs. Our heads are touching. I find myself giggling until I'm red in the face. Something about lying down there, laughing, makes me laugh even more.

'Let me grovel in the dirt while I stand up to you.' Rhiannon joins in. The perspective of the ceiling causes hilarity in me.

'You can't stand up to anyone if you have no backbone, ya big jelly.' Preston reaches over and wobbles Jan's huge stomach.

Breathing deeply, Jan sits up and looks at me. 'That Greg hasn't done anything really that wrong, has he? Has he treated you badly? I mean, he said he had a stalker, and she seems like a stalker.'

Jan is making some sense.

'And maybe Karina messaged him about something minor. He hadn't heard from her for ages, so it wasn't worth mentioning. Perhaps the other woman liked him, since they dated. You had that dentist who liked you, didn't you? And the architect guy? They know your number and can text you? But that doesn't mean you like them better or even at all.'

'I'm warning you. He is a wrong 'un.' Preston sits bolt upright.

'Oh, Preston!' Jan whines.

'I tell you. Men are dogs. D.A.W.G.S,' he continues.

'Oh, are we back on the animal thing again?' Rhiannon says, raising herself to the couch. 'I feel a bit sick.'

Preston stands, his hands on his hips. 'Aye, but I've changed my mind. They aren't dogs. They're worms. Just worms looking for a hole. I have to ask you one thing, Lyssa. Did you sleep with this man?'

'No, something made my shutters go up.'

'Good,' he says, narrowing his eyes and pointing at me. 'Are you sure?'

'I didn't sleep with him,' I bark.

'Good! Keep it that way. If you decide to speak to him again, tell him the vagina shop is closed.'

'I will!'

'And let him know you won't sleep with him until the cows freeze over!'

THIRTY-SEVEN

LYSSA

I WAKE up and nip to the shower. I need to appear fresh. I apply a smidgen of tinted moisturiser, nothing too heavy. I must keep a natural, I-wake-up-like-this look. I brush my hair flat and smooth. I perform all these tasks in silence, almost holding my breath. I can't chance Greg waking up and seeing me.

He kindly offered to help me unpack some boxes that I didn't have the guts to open: personal items, souvenirs of my marriage. I had avoided unpacking them, as I hadn't expected to be here for any length of time. My options remain limited. I could afford another property of this size with my budget, on my own, but it is still a come down. If I married a rich man, I could aim higher. Greg was so kind, so helpful. He made me tea and let me lie on the sofa while he did most of the work in the spare room. I have brushed off all my earlier suspicions as silly nonsense.

The world wants to see post-traumatic growth. It wants happy endings. This is the beginning of mine, I hope. In my worst moments of the last months, people told me I would *learn* from Duncan's death and my grief. As if I could come through it with an education, as if they saw my husband's death as a tool for character development, rather than a tragedy. However, I've moved on in a way by meeting Greg. By *sleeping* with Greg.

I still wrangle fears, but I've entered a new state. I recognise I'm different to before. I have this anxiousness now. I call it post-Duncan paranoia.

I saw a TikTok that said you should acknowledge your fears. I acknowledge it. I will beat it away. However, negative thoughts still keep popping into my head from nowhere, fighting for airspace.

He's like Duncan. No! Just because Duncan did this, does not mean Greg will, Lyssa!

Maybe Louise and Greg are an item. No! she is obsessed with him and wants him all to herself.

I physically shake myself and paint on a smile. Then I slip under the covers and fake sleep.

Greg stirs, and then wakes. 'Morning beautiful,' he murmurs.

'I'll pop in the shower,' I say.

'Cool. Shower time for me after. Then I'll take you to breakfast.' He yawns.

'Thank you.'

'Debbie's, yeah?' He suggests, as I walk to the bathroom.

AS I SHOWER, my mind races again. *Debbie.* Debbie had laughed when I mentioned Greg's name. She knows something, but she's not letting on. I need to find out everything. But how do you ever know *everything* about *everyone*? You can't read people's minds. I leave the shower on for Greg, so he doesn't hear me step back into the bedroom.

'Hey, there,' I say. He has the drawers of the bedside table open. 'What are you looking for?'

'A phone charger. I thought you might have one like mine. I've left mine at home. I wasn't expecting, you know ...'

'Mine is here, plugged in.'

'I'm sure I saw you get one out of here.'

'Does it fit?' I ask. He reaches over and plugs his phone in.

'Yeah, it's perfect, like you.' He gets up and goes to the shower.

I dress, lie back down, and close my eyes, waiting for him. He takes long showers. My eyes open again to see his phone left on the bedside table. I feel my pulse in my neck, and my throat tightens. My hand reaches over almost automatically, and the decision is made.

I'll just check it again.

I see no new texts of interest, and I'm short on time, so I try Facebook. Greg is logged in. The top name on messenger is Robyn Khafoor. I don't open the message, as it hasn't been opened by him, but I see the first line. It was sent three days ago.

I receive messages all the time from admirers. On the whole, they're creeps and weirdos, so I don't open them either. It makes me happy that so much time has passed and he has not replied. But then I remember all the times it took him forty-eight hours or more to answer me. And, of course, a call could have taken place in that time. Or maybe even a meet-up in person. I was out on Saturday, and he was out on Sunday for a meal with Fraser, but I don't know that for sure. He could have been meeting her.

People would say, 'You don't know where he is!' But no one knows for sure where anyone is. They tell you, and you believe it—or you don't.

I can see nothing from Karina or Louise on messenger. Maybe Louise is blocked on that site. Hearing the shower go off, I replace the phone.

ON GREG'S RETURN, I am lying with my eyes closed, although I am awake. I have often practised pretending to sleep beautifully. I lie still, quietly breathing, not snoring or drooling, and with my mouth closed and a hint of a smile.

'Hey there, sleepy. Debbie's now?' He pauses to examine the crucifix on the wall as he dries himself. 'What's this monstrosity?'

'I like it. We liked it. We bought it on holiday. Dunc—' I can't bring myself to say his name while a half-naked man, his friend even —stands in the room.

'You religious, then?'

'A bit. It's a comfort. You?'

Greg has a habit of pontificating. I let him talk, as he looks happy when doing it. 'I would say that if you look at the evidence—science, evolution, and the like—it is hard to believe in religion. Still, it doesn't cost anything to believe. If it is real, then it's a win-win. I'm hedging my bets, if you like. I do not believe in any brand of religion. Instead, I like a bit of this and that. I believe in creation as energy. It doesn't care if we do our own thing. It's not sitting there in judgement. And there is no real wrong or right. All that exists is people doing what they want because it feels good. That is how I think creation, or the Universe, would consider us. You okay?'

'I'm okay,' I lie.

I am not okay. I've not taken in the details of his speech, which probably showed on my face. I am thinking about that message from Robyn K.

Hi darling xx.
How are you today, sexy? xx

THIRTY-EIGHT

RHIANNON

'I CANNOT BELIEVE we are doing this,' I moan, as we roll up on the crunching gravel to the house. The Grand House glistens in the sun after the rain, as if brushed with a recent coat of varnish.

'We are only looking at a house advertised for sale. Anyone can do it.' With a wave of his hand, Preston indicates three other cars in the driveway.

'It's not any old house, Preston. It's Lyssa's old house. She'll be fuming.'

Two men appear at the doorway, pausing my thought thread. They shake hands at the door. The tall one stays, checking his phone, while the short, slim fellow wearing a baseball cap walks away towards the parked cars.

'Well, we aren't telling her ladyship, right?' Preston whispers, and I nod. 'Anyway, I'm not being nosey. I'm looking at it for a different reason. Another angle, it's research.'

I snort, and he glares at me as he opens the car door.

'To me, it's Winifred's house. This is a historical investigation.'

'Historical investigation, my arse. You are looking for any excuse to go running to Sidney with your research. Winifred's been dead years. She won't have left anything behind. No trace.'

'You never know.'

We amble between the cars to the front door.

'I keep seeing green cars. Is it the "in" colour these days?' I mention.

'What? Green, for cars? I wouldn't have thought so.'

The tall, dark-haired man looks up from his phone and bounds towards us, He summons to us to enter, holding the door open to the porch.

'Hi, I'm Tony,' he says in a thick Irish drawl. 'I'm the estate agent you spoke to on the phone. I have the pleasure of showing you around this fabulous property. The executor of the will is a friend of mine, Greg Holstead.' He shakes my hand, and then Preston's firmly. 'Do you know Greg?'

'Oh, aye. We know Greg, all right.' Preston sneers, and I throw him a look.

'Oh, yes?'

'Let's say we know *of* him.' Preston smiles a mealy-mouthed smile.

Tony whirls around to face the grand hallway, where an enormous staircase snakes away from us. I kick Preston in the shins, mouthing, 'Shut up!'

'So, you're here to view this wonderful property. Let's begin. You will love it. Ladies first.' He gestures.

I enter the hallway, the men following closely behind.

Tony leads us through to a swish kitchen, pointing out an office, with many books lining the walls, on the way. 'What did you say your circumstances were? Is your property on the market?'

I gape, not knowing what to say.'

Not yet. But it will be soon.' Preston smiles his lie with a winning grin. I stifle a giggle.

We follow Tony from room to room of the lower floor, nodding and making approving noises at every turn.

'Okay, now I'll let you have a roam, or would you rather I took you upstairs?' He looks straight at me with a glint in his eyes as he says this, and I feel myself blush and swallow hard. Then he turns to Preston with a cheeky smile. Neither Preston nor I speak. Tony doesn't seem put off by our silence; in fact, he seems to revel in it. After what seems an age, he adds, 'Would you prefer to see yourself around?'

Preston and I breathe again, although I still say nothing.

'No ... I mean, yes. We'll be fine.' Preston manages.

'I'll let you explore, then.'

'Thanks.'

Tony's phone rings. 'Ah, I must take that. Do you mind?' he asks, indicating the phone.

'No, not at all.'

'Hello, hello there. Hold on a minute,' he says, his hand over the mouthpiece. 'I'll be in the car if you need me,' he mouths. 'I've a few emails to attend to, if that is okay.'

'Perfect! Thank you! We've looked at the plans online, so we've a fair idea of our way about, Tony,' Preston gushes.

We watch Tony jog off to his car.

'Ooh, I love an Irish accent. He'd just have to say hello, look into my eyes and ... Oh, oops all my clothes fell off!' Preston mimes dropping his clothes to the floor, splaying his arms wide. I feel a blush redden my cheeks. I one hundred per cent agree.

'Concentrate, and let's rake about.'

I feel a thrill building up. I have experience in sneaking around. Perhaps it is an itch I need to scratch again.

We creep about, as if it's not permitted.

'How is the house still furnished with their stuff?' Preston sniffs.

'I guess Lyssa took what she needed and left the rest for wifey number one. Also, it looks better dressed up like a house. Where to?'

'Upstairs.' Preston answers with purpose.

Climbing the staircase, we become aware of another person in a side room. I indicate a ladder leading up to an open hatch and attic space.

'We will get there, by hook or by ladder,' Preston mutters, starting upwards.

'What did you say?'

'Oh, just a saying. Come on!'

'Not sure I've heard that one, Preston,' I mumble, following him. 'What are we looking for anyway?'

'Clues.'

'Clues. What bloody clues? There's only a bunch of boxes. All of them modern.' We fumble about, scrambling over boxes and peering in them.

Preston sighs. 'It's like looking for a needle in a hayride. Look under all the insulation. If you were hiding something, it would be there.'

'They wouldn't have had insulation way back when Winnie died.'

'Okay, but the insulation might have been put on top of things.'

'This is a waste of time!' I whine, frustrated. Standing up fully, I bump my head, curse the rafter, and give it a slap. 'This isn't *Scooby Doo*, you know. Clues aren't going to fall into our lap,' I moan, returning to the hatch.

We hear Tony at the bottom of the ladder. His voice rings out loud and clear, 'Is that you finished there?'

I open my mouth to answer, assuming he is talking to Preston and me, when another voice butts in from below.

'Yes. Yes. I've listed and photographed all the items.'

I hold my breath, as if that will help me to eavesdrop better.

'And you checked the drawers for any paperwork? Mr. Holstead asked me to go through the antique pile for him.'

'Yes, nothing there. I'll get the estimates over to Mr. Holstead by the end of tomorrow.'

'Good, good. I'll let him know,' Tony answers. Then, as I descend the ladder, he says to me, 'Plenty of storage here.'

'Yes, great!' I cringe at my lame reply, but all my concentration is on descending the ladder and on the figure leaving. Glancing at Tony at the bottom, I pull my fingers through my hair, wishing I'd made more of an effort.

'Still got to look round the top floor rooms, Tony,' Preston adds, flashing a grin as he joins me at the base of the ladder.

Tony takes the hint. 'No problem. I'll leave you to it.'

We enter a room off the hall. Preston follows my gaze, taking in a neatly stacked corner of brown furniture, a dressing screen, and smaller items marked with stickers.

Preston barges past me and reads out, 'Musselburgh Museum and Rosewell Auction Rooms. I wouldn't have thought Alyssa would have been much for antique furniture. Maybe Duncan had an interest, or they've just been here a long time.' Preston's eyebrows raise.

'What's that there, in the corner?' I ask. He reaches over and shakes a box.

I grab it from him. 'I can't open it,' I utter, clawing at the lid. 'But I think there's something in here.'

'We'll deal with that later. It's portable. Oh my God! What if the chain around her neck in the painting has a key, and that opens the box? The box is old enough. Take it. Go on! Stick it in your bag.'

'Are you okay up there?' We hear a faint cry from downstairs.

'Shit, the sexy Irish man!' we say together, as we continue arguing in mime.

'You take it.' I stage whisper.

'You take it!'

'Take the bloody thing.'

'Oh, for fuck's sake!'

'Should we take it?'

'Who the hell is gonna miss it?'

'Maybe they will.'

'I told you to bring that rucksack for a reason, Sneaky Sneakerson.'

'I'm not sure.'

'Well, I can't make split-minute decisions for you.'

We both flinch at an Irish accent wafting up again. 'How are you getting on? All good?'

I throw the box back down on the table.

'Yes, thanks. We've seen all we need,' Preston mutters, rushing past the Irishman.

We wave our final goodbyes to Tony from the car.

'Oh, I love a wee adventure,' Preston announces, staring out of the window. 'He's like Peirce Brosnan, eh Rhiannon?'

'A bit,' I reply.

'Can't believe you never took that box,' he moans. Preston puts on his glasses, peering out as I drive past the Irishman. 'But now that I get a right look, he doesn't look like him at all. It's just that accent.'

'And the charm.'

'Yeah. Oh, the charm. He had plenty of that. Okay, he disnae look like him, but I'll call him Pierce anyway.'

'Fair enough.'

'The Pound-shop Pierce.'

THIRTY-NINE

LYSSA

I SIT AT THE TABLE, gazing at Greg's strong back while he talks to Rough-as-guts Julie behind the counter. Christmas songs play, which should be jolly, but for the dreich wet day and the shabby tinsel Debbie has thrown up here and there. My phone buzzes as Greg orders our breakfast and drinks.

I stare at my phone.

'Oh, you're on your phone, I see!' Greg says on his return. 'You sexting, eh?' He grins. He's back to being the cocky, teasing Greg. He seems to have two sides. Gentle Greg of last night has gone.

'It's my phone,' I say, wondering why I said that, but he doesn't seem fazed. Maybe he didn't hear. He appears not to be listening anyhow.

'The minute my back is turned. I know the kind you are!' He laughs as he sits down.

'I'm texting Jill.'

'I know the kind you are, all right,' he says again.

'She was Angela's workmate. Her mum recently died.'

He chuckles.

'Jill, though,' I continue in a bolder tone. '*Her* name is Jill—a *woman.*' I say it louder again. I show him my phone, with Jill's name at the top. He pauses, takes a look, and then shrugs.

'Anyone could be filed under Jill in a text. I'll need to watch you!' He snorts.

I shake my head. My mind flips to his phone. *Darn, I skipped over the messages from male names.*

'Projecting much?' I blurt out. *What am I doing? I don't recognise myself.*

He pauses. 'Meaning?'

'Louise?' The cocky Greg makes me anxious.

His face falls into an expression that reminds me of grey stone.

'I told you about that,' he whispers. He purses his lips and shakes his head. Then he perks up. 'Let's see.' He grabs my phone. 'Who is this?' He scrolls through my gallery of photos. 'Who's that?'

I feel flustered, but I freeze. If I grab my phone, he may imagine I have something to hide.

'My friend's nephew,' I answer to one of his probes.

'Yeah, sure!' His wrinkled smile returns.

Why do men suit wrinkles? It is not fair.

He jumps up and pulls on his coat. Then he reaches down and squeezes my shoulder. I wish he would kiss me in front of Debbie, who is gawping from the back room.

'I have to work. You stay here. Finish your coffee. I've paid already.'

Sighing, I watch him go. The December rain trickles down the windowpane, as I gather my things together to head home.

A woman enters, wrapped up for the cold, and collects a coffee in a paper cup. She leaves, juggling a newspaper, her drink, and popping up her umbrella with one hand. A bottle of wine pokes its neck up from her handbag. I recognise her face, but I can't place her.

I signal to Rough, as she deposits a fried breakfast on the table next door. *Ugh!* The smell of it makes me feel sick. I much prefer sourdough and avocado.

'Who was that woman?' I ask.

'Oh her. Dunno. Comes in most mornings for her hangover coffee,' she shrugs.

'She works with Greg, I think,' Debbie adds, in passing. She glances at her phone and then runs into the back, saying, 'Oh God, the school. I just dropped them off!'

'Oh yes, the grumpy secretary.' I laugh.

'You know her?' Rough asks.

'Sort of. I've seen her.'

'She's not local. Australian, I think.'

'Who're you talking about?' asks Debbie on her return, looking flustered with her car keys in hand.

'The woman who just left. The Australian,' I answer.

'Ah, right! She's not Australian. Louise is from New Zealand.'

FORTY

RHIANNON

'OH HIYA, JULIE!' Preston exclaims in surprise, as she sets down his food. As she dawdles away, I whisper, 'When did Rough start working here?'

'I told Debbie she needed a regular cleaner. She must be doing a wee shift serving. A fine face of the business.'

I stifle a yawn.

'Keeping you up, am I?'

'I was woken up by that Greg banging about.'

'Oh, aye? What's being going on while I've been sleeping?'

'He pressed our flat buzzer late, visiting Lyssa. Did you not hear?'

'Nut, I sleep like the dead.'

'I don't even think she was in. I saw him through the peephole, dashing past.'

'He's coming and going a lot, if you get my drift. Slamming the door and bounding up the stairs like a demented Tigger. I don't always catch him, but I see his fancy silver Mercedes parked in the visitor spot overnight.' Preston changes tack. 'So, what have you today?' He eyes the file I'm removing from my rucksack.

'I now possess this ...!' I brandish my find. 'I raked the archives for her will.'

'Magic! Where there's a will there's a lay.'

'Where there a will there's a slay.'

'Where there's a will, there's a load of relatives.'

'Touché, Preston. You win.'

'Thank you. Go! Let's hear it.'

I clear my throat.

'IN THE NAME OF GOD AMEN. This twenty-first day in May in the year of Our Lord One Thousand Eight Hundred and Forty-six, I Winifred Orr, the widow of Inveresk Parish in the county of Lothian, being of a sound and disposing mind, memory and understanding do make and ordain this my last Will and Testament.

That is to say principally, and first of all, I commend my soul into the hand of Almighty God who gave it and my body I recommend to the earth to be buried in the churchyard of Inveresk in a decent and Christian manner, seven feet at least beneath the surface of the earth at the discretion of my Executor hereinafter to be named.

And, as for and concerning such estate money, goods, chattels, and effects which it hath pleased God to bless me with, I give and dispose of in manner and form following.

And first, if I should choose to marry

again, to my loving husband I give, bequeath
and devise all the land and dwellings at The
Grand House, Inveresk for his natural life.

And if I should not marry, I give, bequeath
and devise the same plot of land and house
abovementioned unto my daughter, Eleanora,
and to her order for and during his own
natural life. And should my daughter,
Eleanora, hereafter be lawfully married and
her husband survive her, I give the
aforesaid dwelling gardens and orchards and
appurtenances including pathway and hedge.

Item: The pathway shall always remain the
width it now is, being at the Entrance Gate
Ten feet and the garden hedge opposite the
right-hand side of the outhouse adjoining
the House. The width of it now is sixteen
feet, and my will is that my daughter,
Eleanora, or whomsoever shall benefit, shall
always keep the hedge well so as not to hang
over the pathway.

The rest residue and remainder of my money,
goods, chattels, and effects as also all
writings of what kind or denomination I give
and bequeath unto my aforesaid daughter,
Eleanora, to equally share between my nieces
and nephew and share alike, nothing doubting
but peace and love will be with them in the
division thereof.

And I do hereby revoke and disannul all and

every other former Testament Wills and Legacies and bequests and executors by me in any way before named willed or bequeathed, ratifying and confirming this and no other to be my last Will and Testament. And I do hereby constitute and appoint Gregory Holstead whole and sole executor of this, my last Will and Testament, unto which, though written with my own hand, I have hereunto subscribed my name and set my seal this twenty-first day of May in the year of Our Lord One Thousand Eight Hundred and Forty-six.

Signed, sealed, published, and delivered by the said **Winifred Orr** *as and for her last Will and Testament in the presence of us, who at his request in his presence and in the presence of each other have subscribed our names as Witnesses thereto.*

Signed: The Mark and seal of **Winifred Orr**
Witnesses: **Charles Smith** *and* **William Glass**
At Musselburgh on the 21st day of May 1846
Gregory Holstead sole Executor above named was duly sworn before me.
Solicitor's name: Gregory Holstead.'

FORTY-ONE

LYSSA

'DO YOU TRUST ME?' he asks, leading me from the underground garage.

'Yes,' I whisper.

'That's a mistake,' he laughs.

Dangerous. Surely, he's joking, trying to act exciting. It's just something funny to say. I'm getting used to Greg's sense of humour. We're at the 'vying for power' stage of our relationship, with neither willing to admit any feelings. He can't let his guard down this early. It's only been weeks, after all.

I want to ask, 'How come your stalker works with you?' I want to question him about Louise, but I can't risk upsetting him. I can't be needy, even if I don't want to risk another failed relationship. He'd wonder how I found out about her. He'd wonder how I knew where she lived.

I'd run out of Debbie's that day to catch Louise sauntering away. I'd followed her to his office, confirming she worked there. Then I'd waited until they finished work, lurking in the vennel with my doggos until I saw the office light switch off. I had watched her walk towards the bridge and turn right, up Eskside. She had entered a set of flats. I scanned the car park for her car until a familiar voice interrupted me. Debbie had walked out of the stairway and was standing beside me.

'Oh, what are you doing here? You don't live here!' I found myself saying.

'My old aunt does.' She pointed to the ground floor flat on the left. 'I check on her most days. Anyway, how are you? You bolted this morning in such a hurry.'

'Oh, fine.'

She reached over and squeezed my arm. 'You are so strong. You know he would have wanted you to be happy. Despite the circumstances, he did love you. It was obvious.'

'Yes.' I have been told these things over and over.

Is everyone read a script of what to say to grieving people? People seem programmed to say such things. *They're in a better place. Remember the good times.* Have they learnt to say those words, watching others say them? Phrases like that are passed down when someone passes over.

I've not been party to the script, so I gawp at her. By luck, we are interrupted by a couple of old dears exiting the building.

'Oh, Auntie Mary!' cries Debbie gesturing to me. 'Auntie, this is Lyssa who I was telling you about. Lyssa, Auntie Mary and Mr. Ross her ... um ... companion.'

We nod a greeting.

'Mr. Ross is taking me for afternoon tea, so we can't stop.'

'Have a lovely time,' I say. We watch Mr. Ross and Auntie Mary spend a ridiculous amount of time getting settled into Mr. Ross's green car.

'You're lucky in a way,' I hear Debbie say.

'Oh?'

'You're young enough to find another partner and move on.'

I force a smile.

'And you know, he wouldn't want you to be sad or live on your own.' She digs further, 'Like Auntie Mary and Mr. Ross.' She tilts her head towards them, still faffing about with the seatbelts. We wave as they eventually leave. No wonder they had no time to chat; the pace they move at.

Debbie prattles on. 'You know, in a way, you should be grateful for the time you spent together.' Another of the usual platitudes rolls off her tongue.

They don't help me. They aren't for me. She says these predictable words for herself. She has had to deal with me, grieving, standing right in front of her. It's quite a situation.

I'd wandered home then, at a dead end. Knowing where Greg's supposed stalker lived helped me none. Plodding up the flat stairs, I remembered what Rhiannon had said about getting information from the electoral roll, and I hastened my step. I bought credit to open up information on sites I'd never heard of before, and my heart thumped, as if I'd get caught doing something I shouldn't. I felt powerful. Clever.

I found out nothing about Louise that I didn't know already. But I did discover that Karina still lives by the bridge. I stared out of the window. I could catch a glimpse of the bridge if I twisted my neck. Both still lived on the exact street, separated by the road leading to the bridge and the river. I searched for Robyn. I found her, too, in an address over the bridge and behind the high street, on Inveresk Road —the road I'd grown up on. All three of Greg's women were within walking distance from where I sat, like points of a triangle! But, of course, I haven't told him any of this.

I SIT IN HIS LIVING-ROOM-CUM-KITCHEN, trying to pull my boots back on as Greg barges about in the bedroom. Cursed with a high instep, I often cannot squash boots around that corner without a struggle. I look up in concentration towards the shelves and notice a bus timetable. Not one, but a pile of them on a shelf. *Why have more than one?* There's also a pile of advert leaflets, flyers for attractions in the area. It looks like a tourist information section to help those on holiday orientate themselves.

Once booted, on impulse I open a drawer, and then another. All empty. *Why?* Why leave items on tables and countertops? I give myself a shake. *Men! They never put anything away.*

I haul open a final drawer in a sideboard. A solitary, crumpled boarding pass. I finger it. Singapore to London Heathrow dated the week Duncan died.

Hearing Greg coming back, I slam the drawer shut and sit back down again. I don't say anything when he enters. My mum and granny would always say, 'She's quiet, but she'll be taking everything in.' They weren't right. Most of the time, I thought of nothing. I was not like I am now, where I can't turn my brain off.

'There is this woman on here,' Greg says, playing with his phone. 'She is married but has not taken her husband's name. Would you take my name?'

There is no right answer to this. I go for the cheeky option, which is often Greg's style after we have spent the night together.

'No, because you'd only be chasing more legal fees,' I joke.

He pouts and lowers his eyebrows.

Should I have said yes? I'm scared to, I realise. Greg doesn't just pull the rug from under me when I open up—he lays the rug down, helps me step on it, and then yanks it from under me, as if laying a trap.

'Ah, you're a Feminazi!' He reverts back to his joshing ways, but his eyes tell a different story.

'No.' I smile.

'Yes, yes! A Feminazi indeed.'

'Have you lived here long?' I change the subject, longing for a normal conversation.

'Off and on.'

It was a pretty flat in Leith, but a flat nonetheless, and no better than the one I resided in. It was not where I thought a successful solicitor would live. His car had suggested a more affluent lifestyle.

But his flat, although pleasant, was average. As if he's read my mind, he says, 'I can afford somewhere fancier if my plan comes together.'

I pause. Greg doesn't say a word, just smirks at me. I'm annoyed that there's no follow-up or explanation. *A plan, what plan?* I could ask, but he'd likely just say, 'Only joking, I've no plan.' Then I'd wish I hadn't asked.

'You've been to Singapore?' I blurt out.

'Yes, yes, I have. Ages ago.'

'Last year?'

'No, the year before.'

Maybe I read the date wrong. It didn't say what year. *Did it?*

Without warning, he pulls me to my feet. 'Right, off you go, then. I'll deliver you home.'

Maybe he'd been embarrassed by the flat, or perhaps irritated at my flippancy after he'd hinted we might be married. Perhaps he felt rejected. I smile at the thought that he does care, that there could be a future for us.

When Greg sees my smile, he kisses me on the forehead. Then he walks away, holds the door open for me, and with his back to me, as if reading my mind again, says, 'Don't spoil what we have with expectations, darling.'

FORTY-TWO

RHIANNON

'SHE'S a helluva bothered about what happens to her bush.'

'Whit?'

'In the will—there's a lot of detail about her hedge. Don't cut this, don't move it here, dinnae over trim my big bush.' Preston sniggers.

'Childish!' I scold, without letting him get another word in. 'So, what have we learned today, Preston?' I peer over my reading glasses. 'From the will? The lawyer fella's name?'

'I didn't catch that. Sorry, I drifted off. It was kinda boring.'

I dangle the document in front of him and sway it from side to side. He grabs the will off me. 'Hold on!' he demands. 'The lawyer's name ... Gregory Holstead.' He says it matter-of-factly, but then jumps up and holds his hands to his face. 'Exact same name as yer man what's dating Lyssa. Is he related? No! It's a coincidence surely.'

'I doubt it.'

'I don't trust that modern Greg. Out to butter his own nest for sure.'

'And?'

'And what?' Preston looks blankly at me and shrugs.

'Who benefits from the will?' I continue.

'Her daughter!' Preston looks pleased with himself.

'Okay, yes, unless Winnie marries again. Or, as it says, the daughter's husband, should the daughter marry.'

'The daughter obviously wasn't married at the time the will was written. If she should marry ... Did she?'

'That I can find out,' I answer. Preston watches as I bring up Eleanora on *Scotland's People* on my phone. I present him with the marriage certificate.

'Et voilà. Guess who Eleanora married the year after Patrick died?'

Preston waves his hands in the air and rises from his seat.

'Calm doon!' I order.

'I'm no' saying anything,' he hisses at me. 'Gregory Holstead, though. They're flocking around like a murder of crows ...!'

I fold my arms.

'I imagine it's the same Gregory that executed the will, the lawyer. Once he knew he could benefit, he married Eleanora.'

'He wouldn't have wanted Patrick marrying Winifred. You think he did Patrick in?'

'It is a jump. He wouldn't have wanted Patrick around, so that would make him a suspect.'

Preston has an elated look on his face. 'Dear me, we have opened up a real box of worms, and all we wanted to find out was how the painting ended up with Patrick.'

'I wonder how he transported it home if he did nick it? It would look a bit obvious, lumping that down the hill. I mean, he didn't just jump on the number 45 bus. How could he have hauled that down the street with no one seeing?'

Rough has been lurking at our table for some time, waiting to take our plates away.

'In the tunnel,' she butts in.

'The what now?'

'The tunnel. Mum used to clean for the owner years ago. I'd go with her in the school holidays. In the drawing room, behind the fireplace, there was a tunnel. I used to play in it. It goes to the town hall and the river.'

It's the most I have ever heard Julie utter. 'Jesus, Rough—I mean, Julie,' I spit out.

'Hold on! There are tunnels under the town? Since when?' Preston stands, and Rough takes his seat as instructed by him. 'Bloody hell! The old town hall is right across the road from the baker's,' Preston adds.

'It's all adding up,' I say.

'There are loads of them around here under the town,' Julie says. 'I remember Mum telling me. Escape tunnels and smuggling ones. One from the river goes two different ways. One part goes up to Fa'side castle, I heard. Some go on to Carberry and Inveresk, like the one I know. One goes to Pinkie House. Mary Queen of Scots lost a ring in one of them. Folks were aye trying to find it. I thought everybody knew.'

Somehow, once Julie gets started talking, you can't stop her.

'Get yer metal detector out, Rhiannon. It's time for another house viewing!' Preston exclaims, pulling on his coat. Call Pound-shop Pierce.'

'Gladly,' I say, licking my lips.

FORTY-THREE

LYSSA

AS WE MAKE our way down to the underground garage on the stairs, I don't speak. I'm wary about saying anything. I could see Greg expanding on the don't-get-carried-away speech. Perhaps he'd mention living together, but if I suggested a property, he'd laugh and say I was jumping the gun. I could even imagine him saying, 'Come on, let me lead you down this dark alley.' Then, when he found me there, exclaiming, 'Oh, what are you doing here?'

Maybe I'm reading significance into something insignificant; that, or I'm picking up all the clues that are right front of my eyes and no one else sees them. Clues like the ones I missed about Duncan. I'm now a student of human behaviour, as if it were a foreign language. I have no experience in his dance of 'read my mind', 'guess my motives'. I don't know the choreography of saying the right thing at the right time anymore. I was perfectly good at that before. Now, I have to actively think before I speak. I need to be aware that when someone says this, they mean that. I wish Greg would talk straighter with me, say what he means, but he talks in riddles, jokes and denials.

I thought I could live with a fun, causal relationship, but I can't. Maybe he isn't a long-term prospect after all. On paper, he's a successful lawyer—charming, perfect husband material. I bet he likes how things are at the moment, with him coming and going as he pleases, but that can't carry on forever. Mind you, he did mention me taking his name. Was that a hint? Was he testing the water? Or was he keeping me hanging on with the idea that I might get my happy ever after?

'So, Lyssa. What're you going to do today?' he asks, snapping me out of my inner debate.

'Walk the dogs. I hate leaving them. I never asked whether you like pets?'

'Like would be an overstatement. I don't hate them. I wouldn't hurt them. There wouldn't be much point.'

I'm not sure he answered my question.

'I've applied for a beauty course—facial aesthetics—so I've some course reading on the agenda. I'm a bit out-of-date with the industry, but I suppose I should venture back into the work market.'

I've no intention of actually working if I can snare a rich husband to take care of me, but my current options are limited, with Greg sitting on the fence.

When he doesn't comment or suggest he looks after me, I witter on, disappointed again. 'Would you believe I also still have boxes to put away. I forgot I'd chucked some in the loft space.'

'Oh, yeah?'

'I don't even know what's in them. A bunch of stuff from the den and from a cupboard under the stairs. I threw it all in together.'

'Hey, I could help you again. It must be difficult to go through all the memories and process all that has happened,' Greg says, as we exit. I stop at the car and stare at him. He is kind after all. 'Yes, I'd like that.'

He squeezes my hand. I feel safe again with him, safe and secure. I know I've been behaving irrationally. It's not his fault Duncan did this to me. Those women I've been concerned about were all well in the past, no doubt. I am his current girlfriend. I am the one he chooses to spend time with; he wouldn't do that if he didn't like me, didn't find me attractive and good company. If he had better options, why bother? He's a busy man, and tired at times, which explains the gaps in our time together. He can't spend every waking minute with me.

Once we're in the car, Greg puts the radio on. 'Let's listen to some music while we drive.' He turns on the ignition, and his Sat Nav fires up.

'Stupid thing!' he barks, as he bashes to turn it off and put the tunes on. In his frustration, he presses random buttons. I laugh. Our age group often have trouble with technology.

'Duncan would always ...' my thoughts trail off as the Sat Nav screen offers the most recent destinations. I clock the top one, and it's all I can do to stop my eyes widening.

Inveresk Road—Robyn's address.

FORTY-FOUR

RHIANNON

'OH, LOOK! WHAT'S THAT?' Preston twists around in his seat as we come to halt at The Grand House.

'A sundial.'

'A what now?' He glances at me, and then back to the object. 'What for?'

'Telling the time with the sun.'

'Oh, what will they think of next.'

'Are you kidding me, Preston?' I peer at his blank expression, but I discern no expression that suggests a joke. I inhale deeply. 'What are we looking for now?'

'We will burn that bridge when we come to it,' he says, whipping off his seatbelt. 'A tunnel, for a start.' He climbs out of the car. Over Preston's shoulder, I spot my main motivation for returning. I feel my heart race as Tony bounds up to the car. He marches right past Preston and straight to me. 'Ah, Rhiannon!'

I feel giddy at him remembering my name—no, more than that, at him uttering my name out loud. He grabs my hand to shake it, but this time, I feel him also graze my cheek with a kiss. I breathe in his aftershave until I believe I might cease breathing altogether.

Grinning, I recognise I'm also reddening like an idiot and pull away. Tony holds my hand for far longer than necessary before releasing my grip and spinning away.

'And Preston, of course.' He jogs over and shakes him by the hand. 'A second viewing, folks. A good sign! We have had a fair bit of interest. Of course, these grander properties do stay on the market for a little longer, so I wouldn't read too much into it. We are hoping for closing bids in a matter of weeks.'

To my part disappointment, Preston says, 'You have a wee rest there to yourself, Tony. Rhiannon and I are happy to have a look on our own again. We know our way around.'

'Of course! You know where I am if you need me,' he smiles his winning smile. I nearly sigh out loud, and I'm sure I am still blushing.

As we walk, Preston talks. 'So, yer man Gregory Holstead, the old version, gets this house with Eleanora, and then what ...?'

'It stays with the Holsteads for another three generations. Greg's dad doesn't inherit it, though. His grandad sells it quite late on in his life to a couple called the Smiths.'

'Righty-ho. So, his family lost the house. Wonder why they moved? Ran out of money?'

'Maybe. Who knows? Greg looks well-to-do, with the Mercedes.'

'Lyssa told me he lived in a flat in Leith—a bit of a come down. Where's all the money gone?'

'Leith is decent enough.'

'Not compared to this gaff.' We pause in the huge living area, gazing at the cornicing. 'Rough said the tunnel was at the back of the fireplace,' I say. We both pause for a second and then dash to the opposite wall.

'The size of the thing, eh?' I wonder, slapping the marble.

'You can climb right in it. Hello! I'm in the fireplace!' Preston waves at me, his head obscured by the mantle.

I join him, tapping around the back until I discover a hollow-sounding noise at a boarded-up section.

'Move that plant pot,' I order, as I cut away the sealant around the edge of the board with my Swiss army knife.

'You're wrecking their house, ya vandal,' Preston whispers, glancing out towards the door.

I hesitate, considering whether to continue. Preston kicks the board with his foot. 'Oops.' He shrugs.

I dislodge the board and slip into the space. Preston follows. Grabbing the flashlight from my rucksack, I then turn it towards the darkness.

'Oh my God!'

'It goes for miles.' I drag the board to cover the gap behind us, and we shuffle onwards. We don't proceed more than ten metres before the roof lowers and we have to stoop. Soon, we are in single file due to it narrowing.

'Ach, it's half full o' water,' Preston moans.

'Turn back. We'll try at the Town Hall end, see if we can find where it comes out.'

In the distant background, we hear a bewildered Tony saying, 'Hello? Hello?'

Giggling, we make our way back. Before we remove the board, we listen, hoping Tony isn't waiting for us. When we peep out, he is nowhere in sight. Hastily, we extricate ourselves from the opening and replace the boarding. In no time, he returns.

'Hi, guys. How did you?' He spins around to check the only doorway into the living area. Preston leans in a casual fashion on the mantelpiece, masking any damage we might have done. I glance at his and then at my dirty shoes and smile brightly at Tony. Our ability to appear innocent, despite the evidence, always impresses me.

'I couldn't find you for a while.'

'Funny, we've been here the whole time.' Preston runs his hand through his hair.

'All okay?'

Preston rushes to Tony's side, guiding him by the arm towards the living room door and hall.

'Yes, yes, yes. We do need a bit more time, though, so if you would be a pet and take a seat in the car for a wee bit longer. We'll come find you when we need you.'

'Um, Tony, do you have a card by the way?' I join Preston at Tony's other side, as we usher him out.

'Indeed I do.' He flourishes his card.

Nice one, Rhiannon. Now I have his number!

Tony seems happy to be left alone. Through the window, I watch as he heads to his car.

'I hate to chase your boyfriend away, but let's dodge about a bit more,' suggests Preston.

I poke my nose into the office. 'This looks like it's been messed up since we were last here,' I comment.

'Oh, aye?

'Some of the books have been shoved off onto the floor.'

'How do you remember details like that? Are you sure?'

'I took photos.' I show him my phone.

'You would. Can you imagine her ever reading a book?' Preston murmurs, fingering a wall of hardbacks that are stacked lying on their side, rather than standing up. He knocks the top one to the floor.

'Oh!' He exclaims, picking it up to replace it. 'Hold on a minute,' he pulls another two out of the way 'What's this? A safe?'

'Leave it,' I say, although my attention has been piqued.

'Nut! And the code?'

I step in front of him. *If we are doing this, we are doing it together.*

'1111.' I fire in.

'Oh, brilliant. We'll be here all year at this rate.'

'How about his date of birth?'

'Duncan's? I dunno that! Hers?'

'I dunno. Oh, yes I do. She is a year younger than me.' I type in her year of birth.

'Try the day and month.'

'Ooh, it was only last month. Nope, not that. The age of the house?'

'What is it?'

'Number above the door—1788.'

'How did you remember that?' he asks, pressing the code in.

'Details are important.'

'Never!' he exclaims in a theatre whisper as he feels the clunk of the lock. On opening the door, he sounds disappointed.

'Just one envelope.' He lifts it and puts it in his pocket without any thought.

'That won't be Winnie's.'

'I realise that, just take it. Don't make the same mistake again!' Preston orders.

'Aye, okay. I understand. I wish I'd taken that box when I had the chance.'

As we make to leave, a familiar car crunches on the driveway gravel. A silver Mercedes spins around the other side of the sundial, allowing us to exit the gate.

FORTY-FIVE

LYSSA

THE INSTRUCTOR STANDS by the screen and points to the anatomy of the face. I try to concentrate. There are so many new things to remember. I've never been much of a scholar.

Unlike Angela, I never felt the need to be academic, but then, she did not have her looks to go on.

All super brainy women are plain. My theory is they are mousey to begin with, so they have to become swots to ensure they survive, as no man would look at them twice.

I realise I need to go back to work, but I must branch out from my usual massages. I'm so out of date, although I've had so much fillers and Botox you'd think I'd be an expert.

Listen Lyssa, listen! I think to myself.

'Your fingers are now demarcating the danger zone, also known as "the triangle of death" or the "danger triangle."'

How dramatic.

'This alarming name comes from the fact that the blood vessels in this part of the face have a direct link to blood vessels close to the brain. There are also crucial structures around the eyes, nose, and mouth you must consider ...'

I consider that not only do people want me to experience grief smoothly, but they also want me to emerge a better person. Everyone tells me to move on, says I need to get over the loss, as if his death is a mountain to be climbed on and over.

Oh, look! It's snowing!

'The Triangle of Death area has your sinuses right behind it, as well as important nerves and blood vessels that are responsible for the blood flowing to the brain.'

The triangle of death. My mind drifts to the three women living in the points of a triangle, each within walking distance of my flat.

'When you pop a pimple in this area, the skin might become infected. This infection could spread through to these important blood vessels.'

Grief still spreads through my body. *I'm not over it.* People talk like it's a challenge to overcome. They fail to accept that grief is not separate, not an out-of-body experience; it exists within me. Wherever I go, it follows.

'When that happens, the veins located behind your eyes may clot, putting pressure on the brain, which can have lethal consequences.'

The triangle ladies could cause death. Why does my brain jump to this instead of the lecture? It's like school all over again, no fun at all.

'It's known as Cavernous Sinus Thrombosis, and it can be caused by something as simple as squeezing spots or plucking your nose hairs.'

Yuck!

AT LAST, it ends. I find myself walking back from the course and passing the block I live in. Instead, I stride towards the bridge. I turn to the first point of the triangle: outside Karina's flat. I sit on a bench with my back to her unit, facing the river. I spot an inscription. *In Memory of Agnes Moleman*—my lovely primary school teacher. Bless her. I was always her favourite. It makes me smile to think about her. Then it jumps into my head that one of Greg's women could be looking out of her window at me, burning the back of my neck with her eyes.

Karina has been missing from Greg's texts for weeks now, so she feels less of a threat. I saunter over the bridge and up to the street behind the High Street to where Robyn lives. *Great, big fat Robyn.* My lip curls. *What on Earth does he see in her? She's young, I suppose, but still enormous.*

I'm in Inveresk Road, where I grew up. When people at school asked where I lived, I'd leave out the word road and simply say, 'Inveresk.' They all assumed we lived in Inveresk Village, with the huge houses where prestigious people stayed. I manifested myself living there, I said it so often. They wouldn't consider I could live in the less fancy road at the bottom of the hill, with all the terraced red-sandstone houses.

I remember I once brought a pal back from school to visit. When she saw my house, she said, 'Wow, your house is so small.' I never brought anyone home again. I was so embarrassed. With luck, she did not tell anyone, so it did not affect my popularity.

Angela was never popular—always weird and awkward with a chip on her shoulder. She liked The Pogues and Goodbye Mr. Mackenzie, none of the good-looking bands I liked, like Duran Duran. She always had to be different. It made me angry.

What was wrong with her? I feel angry at her all over again, and then mad at her dying. *How could she?* I walk away with tears streaming down my face. I hope no one sees, but not many people are loitering, as the snow is floating down again. Only that baseball-cap man I keep seeing gives me a second glance.

Marching on, I find myself on the bridge out front of Louise's flat. I have to pass it on my way home. *Home*—I hate calling it that. It is Angela's flat. *My beautiful home is gone now.* I realise I've walked the whole triangle of death.

Debbie told me Louise lived on the top floor and sometimes

parked her green car in the car park but mainly parked in the street, as she struggled to squeeze into the tight space. I couldn't probe Debbie more without sounding suspicious.

I scan the street, seeing a green car. I take a photo of its registration as I stroll by. A frumpy grey cardigan adorns the back seat, and a newspaper—the *Telegraph*—sits on the parcel shelf. It has been there a while; the headline is out of date and the corners are sun-yellowed.

When another green car rolls up and parks right at the flats, I consider I have it wrong. *Maybe this new one is her car.* I burl around and head under the bridge, like a troll, into the underpass. It would be an easy way to cross the street to Karina's place, should I ever need to.

Why would I need to?

I wait. A cyclist passes. The car takes a stupid amount of time to park. Reverse. Come out. Reverse again. I feel awkward lingering, but no one else enters the underpass to see me.

After what seems like an age, an old man gets out of the green car, checks his parking once more, and opens the door for Debbie's Auntie Mary. *What was his name? Her boyfriend? Mr. Ross.*

Greg always opens the door for me like that. *And all the others probably.*

Louise's car must be the first one after all. I walk along the block and back until I have taken seven photos of the area. I'm not sure what to do with them. But I have them, and no one knows. It reminds me of looking at Greg's phone and creeping about on the internet. It excites me. I don't like others knowing things all the time and me being in the dark like I'm stupid. I prefer this, knowing more than them.

I have to do something about these women. I peer up to Louise's flat, which I assume is the one with the light on. Then I look down again at her car. My gaze takes in the newspaper on the back shelf.

And I know what I have to do.

FORTY-SIX

RHIANNON

THE INTENSITY of my stare almost burns a hole in the envelope I hold in my hand.

'Open it!' Preston demands.

'No. We are getting rid of this as soon as possible' I slap it down on my desk. He sticks his lower lip out in a pleading manner.

'No, Preston. Stolen property. Why we took it, I don't know.'

'To make up for your earlier mistake of not taking that box! Well, we'll never know what was in that now.' He slumps back against the wall by my bed.

'No reason to call Sidney, huh?'

'And you've no reason to call Tony for other viewings.' His fingers make quotation marks around the word "viewings".

'The police could be at the door for us in ... 5 ... 4 ...'

'It doubt it. It's not that big a deal,' he mutters, picking fluff off his jumper.

'Theft? Safe breaking?'

'Who's gonna know? Gonna notice?'

'I didn't check for CCTV,' I mumble and then purse my lips. I'm becoming careless.

'In a home office? No, yer paranoid!' He giggles, and I join in.

'I dunno what you're laughing at. The cops are coming for you. You'll be banged up in ten minutes with your record. You are on probation, remember?'

Preston giggles, but then he bites his lip.

'We could fire the envelope under Lyssa's door and no one would know where it came from. Then it'd be returned to its owner.'

'And Lyssa tells Greg. He adds one and one together, as he surely saw us there, and what a coincidence it is suddenly in the flat above where we live.'

Preston takes a deep breath in and holds it.

The flat entry buzzer fires, and I grab Preston. He steps to the intercom, lifts the receiver and presses the enter button.

'You let them in, Preston!'

'I always do that. It was automatic.' He flaps.

'You're meant to ask who it is first!'

'But I never can make people out over the intercom. It's usually Amazon for somebody.'

'Why are we whispering?'

'I don't know.'

'Well, you've let them in the stair. It could be...' We both gaze toward the door until I come to my senses and reach over to click the lock.

We crowd at the peephole. I can't see for Preston's big head. We both hear footsteps coming closer.

'Oh, I can't look!' squeaks Preston, stepping away as the handle jiggles.

I recoil and stare at the handle, pushing Preston forward to step up to the peephole, with the door handle still rattling. His shoulder drops, and as he opens the door, I gasp.

FORTY-SEVEN

RHIANNON

'HI JAN,' Preston says.

'Hi. Why was the door locked? Sorry I'm late.'

'Christ! We forgot you were coming.' I spin and throw myself down into my desk chair.

'I couldn't exit off the A1. I needed to go to the next exit. The one I wanted was closed up. I've been on a tour of East Edinburgh trying to get here. Open that bottle. I need it.' She hands over a gin bottle.

'Yes, we need it, too.' Preston clutches the bottle to his chest.

'I need a clear head, thanks.' I press my fingers to my temples.

'Not me. I need a large one.' Preston sits himself down on the end of my bed, tearing at the plastic around the stopper

'I couldn't see what was going on at the junction.' Jan leans against the doorframe

'It's been like that since yesterday. I saw something on the newspaper site about an accident,' Preston suggests, still fiddling with the bottle.

Jan clearly has not noticed any tension in the air, but it clenches my stomach, making it growl.

'I'm gonna Google it for Terry, who's picking me up later. Is it okay if I leave my car in your visitor's space if I'm having a drink?' Jan carries on as she taps into her phone. Preston nods.

'What's new with you guys anyway?'

'Nothing,' we both say. We are uncharacteristically quiet.

'Oh, here we go.' She shows us her phone. I scan the article.

MAN DIES AFTER HIT-AND-RUN ON SCOTS STREET, AS COPS HUNT FOR SUSPECT VEHICLE

A 57-year-old man's body was found on the A199 at the junction with the A1 between Wallyford and Tranent at around 1.30am on Thursday.

Emergency services were called to the scene in the early hours of Thursday morning, with a 57-year-old man pronounced dead a short time later and officers locking down the area.

The road between Strawberry Corner and the slip road on and off the A1 at this junction remains closed while police attempt to locate the vehicle involved.

A statement from Police Scotland said: "Around 1.30am on Thursday 11 April police were called to the A199 and A1 junction following a report of a suspected fatal hit-and-run involving a 57-year-old male pedestrian. A man's body was found at the scene and enquiries to establish the full circumstances and identify the vehicle of impact, described as a green car, are ongoing.

Anyone with information is urged to contact police on 101, quoting incident 0210 of 11 April.

'Poor bugger. I feel bad now, moaning about my delay. I'll fetch glasses. Are we going to sit in your room all night, Rhiannon?'

'No, no. Let's go through. We'll come through in a minute.' I gesture for her to lead the way and hand her phone back to her. Jan ambles on to the kitchen area.

'Should we give Lyssa a shout to come down?' Jan butts in, stopping in her tracks.

'No!' Both of us reply abruptly.

'No.' Jan shrugs and toddles on.

'Shall we tell Jan about the safe?' I whisper to Preston, hanging onto his arm.

'No. Keep it between us for now. Let it settle. She doesn't need to know any of all this. She'd never keep her trap shut.'

We head towards to the living area, but I gasp and skip back to the front door. 'We'll keep it locked from now on. Right?' I suggest, when Preston glances back at me.

'Oh, hell no!' We hear Jan exclaim from the living room.

'What is it? What is it now?' Preston is static in the hall between us, looking upward, as if speaking to God.

'A new update on the *East Lothian Courier* Facebook page,' Jan cries back. 'You'll never believe who was killed in that hit-and-run!'

FORTY-EIGHT

LYSSA

HE IS VERY LATE TONIGHT.

Yesterday's *Telegraph* newspaper I bought in Portobello draws my attention when I turn away from the window, the streetlights still glimmering in the darkness. I should tidy the flat. For some reason, it gets messed up in no time. I am used to having help, I suppose. But even when I search for the scissors, I notice drawers I have organised before all in a kerfuffle.

I miss being able to tell Duncan something, anything. He was the first person I'd call when something happened, my go-to support person. It didn't have to be something big, like an emergency. Just a small something was enough, like someone annoying me at the tennis club. He knew how long to let me vent for, and how to calm me down. There are times when I still pick up the phone to call him after a terrible day, only to remind myself that he's gone. I couldn't tell him this, though. I *can't* tell him this, as he is dead. I can't tell anyone this, ever.

I've been outside Louise's flat several times now. Her car, her frumpy cardigan, and the newspaper on her back dash haven't moved. She clearly doesn't tidy out her car often. I suppose she doesn't use it much, with working around the corner. I spread my newspaper on the kitchen table and cut out the letters I need. I fashion them onto the page and glue them down. I'm going old school.

I chop the paper up a bit more and place the shredded remains into a clear carrier bag. My crafting is all tidied up well before he arrives.

'HELLO, my lovely. I'm celebrating tonight. A good deal is done. I did a good bit of business. Oh yes, I did.' He brandishes a bottle of champagne, but I'm aware he has already been drinking. He has whiskey lips.

'Uh-huh,' he babbles on. 'Unfortunately, it fucked someone else up, but winner takes it all, as the song goes.' He smiles.

'Oh dear,' I say.

He searches through my kitchen drawers, swaying. 'Darling, you are too sensitive and sweet to succeed in business proper. You need a harder heart. The drive to get ahead, you know.'

'Fucked them up? Wasn't it bad, what you did?'

He seems to like me wanting to know more. 'You see, this is how I view things.' He prattles on, popping the cork on the bottle. 'Everyone has the chance to get ahead. It's all a game.'

He opens the cupboard door and retrieves two Edinburgh crystal champagne flutes.

'This person? Did you not like them?'

'Honestly, you'd have to go through some serious effort to piss me off. As long as I keep myself entertained or circumstances work out to my benefit, it is all good—and, boy, did I benefit tonight?' He grabs me around the waist and kisses me hard. 'Oh yes I did.' He grinds against me.

'You are in some mood. I hope you weren't unkind.'

He snorts. Then asks, 'The question is are you going to be kind to me?'

'Oh, yes.' I smile.

'You are so amenable, my darling little compliant flower.'

I blush as Greg hauls me up to the bedroom with one hand; the two flutes and the champagne bottle in the other.

FORTY-NINE

RHIANNON

ALEX SPENCER'S Funeral Directors announce on Facebook:

It is with heavy hearts that the family announce that Musselburgh stalwart Fraser McIntyre, aged 57, has passed away suddenly following a road traffic accident on Thursday April 10th.

The family appreciates the messages of concern and sympathy but asks that you allow them some privacy to grieve at this difficult time. Funeral details will follow in due course.

Dozens of tributes poured in below the announcement.

'R.I.P Fraser, you were one in a million with a heart of gold.'

'Fraser was a lovely guy and we have so many great memories as children. Fly high, Fraser.'

'So sorry to hear mate. I didn't know Fraser that well but when he passed my door, by the racecourse, he never once passed without saying hello. A true gent.'

Dozens of others sent messages of condolence to Mr. McIntyre's family.

'Are you sure he was the hit-and-run, Jan? Not another accident?' I ask.

'It was only a day ago. That's why the road was closed, and there are more comments underneath,' Jan answers.

'Let's see.' Preston swipes the phone from her and reads the comments out as if reading a shopping list, with one hand on hip.

'I hope the police catch the bastard.

'What a yellow-livered coward to leave him by the road.

'Who would do that? It's awful and you don't know if he would have made it if they just owned up.

'It must be terrible for the family.'

'No one saw anything,' Jan says, her arms crossed as if hugging herself.

'I'll need to phone Terry.' Jan stands up. 'He knew him from the golf club. He'll be devastated.' She takes her phone and walks through to the hall, leaving us alone. Preston and I converse in low voices, as close as we can stand.

'Get that envelope into the drawer out of the way. We'll decide what to do with it later.'

'Poor Fraser, eh?'

'A green car,' I muse. 'I keep seeing a green car. There's one been hanging around our car park and out on the road there.'

'Oh, right.' Preston has a bewildered look on his face.

I continue, 'And there was one at The Grand House, too.'

'Oh yeah, you mentioned it. Must have been either Tony's or the evaluator chap.'

'Or the man who was speaking to Tony when we arrived.'

'I don't remember him.'

'I do. A thin fellow wearing a baseball cap.'

FIFTY

LYSSA

WHEN I VENTURE OUT, it's still dark. I've decided the best way to blend in is to wear a high-vis jacket in the early hours of the morning and tuck my hair into a beanie hat. People won't mention seeing a tradesperson; they won't see it as suspicious. No one looks when you're service personnel. I know I don't pay any attention to workmen and the like. That class of person disappears, even when they're right in front of me.

I change into my disguise in the underpass and stride to Robyn's address, carrying a plain tote bag. I place the plain white envelope through the letterbox. Her ground floor villa with its main door is a gift.

Then I dart across the street, my heart thumping. I march away. *Not too fast now, Lyssa!*

I take the long way back, to avoid passing her door again. I don't want to chance her looking out and catching me running. But I can't help but speed. *What a thrill!* I giggle, and then bite my lip. I pace myself. Robyn should come to the conclusion that Louise is the sender. I don't doubt for a second that Greg's stalker would have interfered in any relationship he had. Surely, he would have bad mouthed Louise to Robyn, like he did to me. I hope he doesn't speak of me that way, if he ever mentions me at all. I am always kind and accepting of his behaviour.

'You are so compliant,' he often says.

'Thank you,' is all I ever respond—the correct reply to a compliment.

Now, for part two. I return to the underpass under the bridge. It is still quiet. I emerge and try Louise's car door. *Yes!* I'd checked last week, and the idiot has a habit of leaving it unlocked. I stash the clear bag of paper cuttings under her shabby old cardigan. I am back in the underpass in seconds, where I change out of my high-vis and beanie. I can't be seen entering my flats with that garb on.

Louise's actions didn't make Greg love her, and mine might not either. Perhaps nothing would settle Greg to loving anyone, but it feels like my only chance to get these others out of the way.

Later, I do my regular check of Greg's phone while he sleeps.

> **Robyn: I can't see you again.**
> **This Louise thing has gone too far,**
> **first the tyres let down, now this.**
> **I'm going to the police. I've had enough.**
> **I've my child to think of.**

I breathe in deeply, clutching his phone to my chest, with Greg sleeping right beside me. I hate these secrets, but he isn't telling me about all his wee conversations with Robyn. Louise's stalking is clear here. Letting tyres down is dangerous.

I jump as the phone vibrates against my body and lights up. I glance over at Greg, still soundly snoring.

Who is calling in the middle of the night? I decline the call, and then delete the record. I thought she was an old threat, with things over between them years ago, but no...! There she is, brazen as the day, the witch.

The phone buzzes again—a text this time.

**Karina: Can we talk???
Why won't you answer me?**

Will she not leave him alone? Now I have her to deal with, too!

FIFTY-ONE

RHIANNON

'IT'S ITEM NUMBER SEVENTY-FIVE. The last item.'

'What number are we at now?'

'Fifty-seven.'

'Jeez. We've been here forever already,' I moan.

'Have you got anything better to do?' Preston questions.

I say nothing, as he knows the answer. I mull over my schedule of visiting Mum and how this auction has got me out of it until tomorrow at least. Sometimes, I wonder if Preston's company is the only thing keeping me going.

'How much are we prepared to pay for a box from a house that means nothing to us?' He muses, hand on chin. His motivation isn't even clear to himself.

'Apart from that it might contain something that could give us information about a painting that we've already been told is worthless,' I add.

'Maybe Sidney is wrong about its value.' Preston throws in, with a flick of his hand.

'Your sainted Sidney! Never!'

He responds only with a harrumph noise before taking a different tack. 'Can I just clarify when I say *we* are paying for it ...' He pauses for my reaction, but gets none, as I deduce what is coming. 'I'm just putting it out there that you are an accountant versus me being a mere café worker.'

'Any more than forty quid and I'm out.' I fold my arms.

'You'll go fifty.' Preston leans back in his chair, and we hear the auctioneer begin.

'Item number seventy-five. A wooden carved box from The Grand House in Inveresk Village. Believed to be from the early eighteen hundreds. No key and currently locked. Sold as seen. Starting bid ten pounds. Gentleman at the back.'

I strain to see behind me.

'Put your paddle up,' Preston stage whispers.

I comply.

'Fifteen.' The auctioneer points to me.

'And twenty, to the gentleman at the back. Twenty-five—lady at the front. And thirty.'

'Who is it bidding against us?' I nip at Preston, swinging my paddle up once more, feeling a tingle of excitement.

'Thirty-five.'

Preston twists his body and shrugs.

'Go see. Go on. Go see. I'll keep bidding.' I feel thrilled. I'm glad I came. Any emotion other than tedium is my drug.

'Forty.'

'I'll go to the toilet and have a look.' He stands as I bid again.

'Fifty.'

'Try no' wave your hands in the air,' I say, as he goes.

'Fifty to the gentleman.'

I pause.

'Going once ...' I hate getting beaten. I throw my paddle in the air and then grasp it back to my body.

'Fifty-five to the lady.'

Immediate guilt hits me. I might end up spending all that money on a stupid box.

'Sixty to the gentleman.'

I clench my teeth. *It's just a box.*

'Going, going ... gone'.

Preston returns and glares at me.

'It was too dear,' I explain, not looking him in the eye. 'Who was it anyway?'

'Some Chinese fella at the back. It was probably worth something. He certainly made sure he got it.'

'Probably a dealer or something. It was getting out of hand. He wasn't giving up.'

Preston sneers. We trundle to the exit and sit in the car. I sigh, as I throw myself down on the driver's seat.

'What now?' Preston asks.

'Nothing. It's a lot of guff anyway. About time we forgot all this nonsense. Here's another thing: we'll tear up that envelope out the house and forget the whole event.'

'That's him that got the box, there.' Preston gestures to a fellow carrying the very box, as I start the engine.

'Him there? Wearing the baseball cap?'

'Yeah, the wee Chinese guy.'

'You don't know he's Chinese. You have to say Asian nowadays. That's the chap who was at The Grand House when we were there the second time.'

'Well, he could have saved himself sixty smackers if he'd been a bit more light-fingered. Must be a bit like yourself. A bottler.'

I give him a tight-lipped smile. We watch as the man enters his car.

'Oh, so the green car isn't Tony's or the evaluator's—it's his!' I say aloud.

'Follow him!' Preston demands, as the green car sails past us.

'What? Why?' I reply, but I follow orders, shifting into gear.

'Oh, why not? Have some excitement in your life. Remember I'm a nosey bugger. Something is up. Someone else is hanging round the big house, wanting the same item we did. And it could be the same car that has been hanging around our flats.'

'I suppose we could follow him and see if there is damage to his car.'

'Ooh yeah, that hit-and-run was a green car.'

'Bloody hell! It's like we are going home anyway, the way he is going. Maybe he's planning to park in our car park again.'

'Better not. I've warned Neighbourhood Watch downstairs,' I mutter.

The green car spins past The Grand House

'I thought for a minute he was taking the box back.'

Instead, the car turns down the hill from the village, and then takes a left at the junction before turning into a driveway in Inveresk Road, parking in front of the modest red-brick villas. I park across the way, in a side street. We observe as he rings the bell. A voluptuous black woman lets him in.

'The car doesn't look damaged from here,' I mumble.

'He could have had it fixed.'

'True. What now?'

'All we wanted to know was whether there was any information about Winfred in there. That's all. Harmless historical interest. Instead, we're wondering why he's been hanging around us all the time, and what he's up to.'

'Well, we'll never know that.'

'There's nothing illegal about asking,' Preston states, unbuckling his seatbelt. I flap around for my bag and phone, but he is off, leaving me trailing behind. The traffic stops me crossing the road. I watch as Preston rings the doorbell and waits. Within a minute, the door opens.

FIFTY-TWO

LYSSA

Earlier that day

WHEN ALL IS CLEAR, I press the service button at Karina's flat. It buzzes and clicks to let me in straightaway. I've made up another *Telegraph* newspaper letter for Karina. I need to scare her off, too. There's some obvious close contact between Greg and her that needs dealt with. My plan worked with Robyn, so there's no need to switch it up.

Karina's flat is more of a rat run than Robyn's, with a chance of meeting a number of residents in the stair. However, in and out I go in seconds; then, it's just a quick dart across the road into the underpass. No standing by the road, waiting for the traffic to calm. No chance for anyone to look out and see me there.

Once there, I remove the high-vis vest and beanie, deposit them in the nearest bin, and shake out my hair. I take the trip over to Louise's flat, up the slope where a community garden sits on the right. I'm halfway there when I peer through the rusty mesh of the fence to spot a police car outside her block. I stop, glancing back. Seeing no one, I wait.

Two police officers exit the flats. I've never been scared of the police before, but now I am quivering. They drive off.

For God's sake! Look in the car! Idiots. The *Telegraph* sits there still with the immovable grey cardigan and the bag underneath.

This isn't going to be enough, and I'm annoyed. Maybe I've scared her off for a while. but I want her out of the way for good. She has been a persistent problem. I retreat, raid the bin for my disguise, stuff it into my tote, and make my way back to my flat.

I SEARCH a couple of boxes that I thought were unopened. It turns out the tape has already been removed, which perplexes me. No doubt it was one of Greg's attempts to help out, but nothing has been emptied from them. I'm sure a set of knives is in one. My good set: the Zwilling ones that I never used, as they were more for show. I take one, clean it, and wrap it in a napkin. Then I place it in my tote.

I check my watch, noting the date: 15 April. It's a special date, my wedding anniversary. It's the anniversary of the thing that never happened. But memories can't die, can they? It felt so real at the time. My whole identity was Duncan's Whatmore's wife. Now that I have to live on my own, who am I?

I stare at myself in the full-length mirror by the door. I am a middle-aged, flat-dwelling, trainee beautician who stalks women. My heart sinks. My head drops. Anger rises from my toes. I want to feel like happy Lyssa again.

I must get rid of these women. There's a chance for Greg and me to happy together, a chance for me to be Greg's special lady, his wife. *To be someone again.*

I grip the knife from outside the cloth bag, to check I still have it. Then I go.

IT'S STILL EARLY ENOUGH NOT to arouse suspicion. People are about, but I can't wait. I change in the public toilets on my way to Robyn's.

She was brave enough to report Louise to the police for a letter. Let's see how she deals with this.

The grammar school pupils traipse to the school building around the corner. In the half-crowd, I take a chance that I won't be noticed. Either a dead street or a crowded one are best to avoid being seen.

I take the few steps to Robyn's front door and deliver the knife parcel through the letterbox. Then I join the uniformed children in walking away, back to the toilets to shake my hair, dump the disguise for good, and head home to prepare for Greg.

FIFTY-THREE

RHIANNON

I SCUTTLE OVER THE ROAD, bag flailing in time to hear the black woman at the door say, 'Come in.'

Preston steps up and gestures for me to join him. I spy the Asian man behind her, lurking in the hall.

'Are you sure about this, Ike?' She asks in an accent that is African in origin.

'Yes, they are harmless,' he replies. I struggle to place his accent. It doesn't seem Chinese, but more sing-song in intonation. I smirk at Preston's assumption.

'Come through,' she says, leading us to a modest sitting room with some playthings in the corner.

'I'm Robyn. This is my house.'

'I'm Preston. This is Rhiannon.' Preston shakes her hand. I nod. Then we sit on the sofa. *What the hell are we doing here?*

The Asian man leans against a sideboard, as Robyn curls her legs up on an armchair opposite us.

'I know who you are. My name is Ikan Haring Merah.' He makes a little bow. 'Call me Ike—everyone in Edinburgh does. You will be wondering how I know who you are?'

'You've been around, in the green car,' I say. We glance to the car in the driveway, visible through the bay window. My eyes linger on it for a few seconds to check it again. *Not a scratch on it.*

'Yes. Maybe a bit conspicuous. You were wanting to know about the box, Mr. Preston.' He places it on the coffee table. 'I wonder do you have a reason for this, like me?'

'Yes, we do.' Preston begins to open his mouth and expand on that, but I press my foot onto his.

'To do with Duncan Whatmore's death, perhaps?' Ike continues.

I nod. Preston's gaze darts to me, and he bares his teeth, as if only a jaw clench would stop him blabbing.

'Maybe we are investigation the same situation. I will be explaining. My cousin back home in Singapore is Kwai Tan, Duncan's wife. I work in Edinburgh in a restaurant. Kwai Tan was not left anything in his will. Instead, he has second wife here, who be inheriting everything.'

'No, that's not right,' butts in Preston, unable to contain himself any longer.

Ike tips his head but carries on. 'The lady moves into your flat block above you, into the flat of her dead sister, until the house is sold, I think.'

Preston shakes his head, which Ike ignores.

'But then Mr. Tony. You know Mr. Tony?'

I blush at his name. 'Yes, we know him. He's lovely, isn't he?' I grin like a schoolgirl.

'Mr. Tony tells me it is Mr. Greg selling the house for Kwai Tan. I did not tell him who I was. He is very chatty, Mr. Tony, but I know this is not true.'

Preston puts his hand up, as if at school. 'Lyssa, his wife, was left nothing. We thought your cousin inherited everything. That's what we thought.'

Ike does not miss a beat. 'I have been checking out first the house, to see if there is another will or any information, and also watching Mr. Greg. He must know what is happening.'

'That's why you've been in our street?'

'Yes, his office is across the street, and Mr. Greg is now boyfriend of Mrs. Lyssa, I see. We do not know how much she knows.'

Robyn shifts in her seat and coughs. Ike straightens from his leaning position and nods towards her. 'Miss Robyn here knows what I am doing. I followed him here, too. He is not a good man. Very much for the ladies.'

Robyn snorts. 'More like the money. He wanted me to put his name on this house, said we could set up a business together. He must think me stupid. My husband left it for me and my boy.'

'We think his other woman, Miss Louise, has threatened Miss Robyn. Just this morning, a knife was put through her door.'

'My tyres were let down, and Greg blamed her, says she's a stalker.' Robyn sits upright and grips her cardigan.

It dawns on me that this was one of the women Lyssa came up with on Greg's phone one night at ours.

'But he is spending time with Miss Louise,' Ike continues.

'Did you see her?' I'm always interested how much people notice others' movements.

'No, it was very early,' Robyn answers. Ike shakes his head.

'I was working late last night. Miss Robyn has been suspicious of Mr. Greg for a while. His motivations and hints of other women. She is wanting to break up with him, but she has been trying to keep in touch to get information for me.'

I take a breath in. 'I have to be honest.'

Preston's eyes widen. 'We were looking into a painting we discovered. We worked out the subject was a lady who lived in the house years ago. We wondered if there was information in the box about it. So, you see, our interest isn't regarding Duncan or Alyssa, but we will help you if we can.'

'I see.'

My eyes are drawn to the object on the coffee table.

'You would like to see the box? We should open it now, yes?'

FIFTY-FOUR

LYSSA

I SETTLE on the living room sofa, doggos curled up at my feet and the last of the champagne in a flute in my hand. I'd sipped a little in the bedroom but tipped most out into the bathroom sink. Greg guzzled his, so I've opened another bottle for him from my house store.

I suggest a film and let him pick. It begins with a cold opening—a stabbing. I jump, and he laughs at me as a montage of pre-credits roll up, setting the scene in Seattle.

'How would you feel if a person was stabbed right in front of you?' I ask, believing my shock was reasonable.

'I wouldn't care.'

'You'd help, though?'

'I might. If I'd benefit, but if not, I'd stroll on by.'

'You wouldn't feel upset or shocked by it?'

'No, why would I? It's not *me* getting stabbed.' He snorts. We watch to the end of the film in silence.

'He was some guy,' I comment, plumping up my cushion.

'Yeah, I liked him.'

'What? Are you kidding? He was horrible to that girl.'

'No, no. She was far too clingy.'

'She liked him—*loved* him even.'

'And he did not like her. Reminds me of Louise. Won't take the hint.' He guffaws.

'I felt sorry for her,' I say, pouring him more wine as he talks.

'She took that as, we were to be together *for-evah*,' he emphasises. 'The thing about Louise is her love, as you call it, is transactional. You know what? I'll tell you a story about her.' He sits up, tittering to himself. 'She bought me a tie once. I didn't have anything to do with her for a while, and I started seeing other people. Then, one day, I was randomly pushed from the back. She almost strangled me, pulling the tie off me. "You aren't having my tie!"' He mimics her in a high-pitched feminine voice and continues, 'You see, she couldn't just gift me anything. She always wanted something in return. Her so-called love is very conditional.'

'But he would call her up, the guy in the film.'

'I've done that with women who are convenient, you know. I went out with another woman not that long ago. She tried to keep in touch with me, and I was always civil with her. I was flattered by her attentions, but she was never a girlfriend. More a friend with benefits.'

I feel myself cringe at the phrase, but I won't let it show on my face.

Greg babbles on, 'She was younger, too, so it did my ego no harm.'

I can see he is enjoying this, considering it braggable behaviour. He must mean Robyn.

When he finishes his wine and falls asleep on the couch, I check his phone, more out of habit than anything else. No texts from any of them. I have won.

But what have I won? Greg?

I look at him, drooling and dishevelled on the sofa. Those women are out of our equation because I scared them off, not because he did not want them. After our conversation, I wonder if he's the booby prize. If they handed me that, I'd ask for a redraw. They could take the prize back and give it to someone else, like the box of unwanted bath salts that does the rounds at every local raffle.

I CAN'T SLEEP, so I tidy up. I take two glasses of water to the bedside table and leave some painkillers on his side. He'll need them in the morning.

Returning to the living area, I curl up on the armchair with a cup of chamomile tea, wondering whether to leave him where he lies. He coughs and stirs, so I help him up the stairs. He flops onto the bed, fully clothed. That will have to do.

He looks vulnerable, quite adorable really. I fetch my drink from downstairs and scroll my phone, looking at my Facebook newsfeed. A post catches my eye.

MUSSELBURGH FOLKS

Anyone know what is going on at Eskside? Police cars parked outside for ages now.

I raid the comments section.

'My aunt says they are at a flat on the top floor,' Debbie comments.

'Bunch of curtain twitchers! Mind your own business!' snarls another.

'They were searching a car in the road when I passed with the dog!'

I pace up and down. *This is all my doing. What if they find out I was behind it?* I never considered that. I am upset that I was driven to this. *The knife with Robyn was too far.*

I return to the bedroom and touch the crucifix, praying aloud with my eyes shut, facing the wall. 'Please, Jesus. I repent. Please help me not let them get to me anymore. Let me turn the other cheek in future.'

I hear Greg laugh at my mumbling. He has arisen again.

'Who are you talking to now?' He grunts.

Embarrassed, I stare at the inanimate object I'm having an intimate conversation with. *What is it anyway? A relic.*

'A relic from my failed relationship,' I say. 'I'm being silly.'

I take it off the wall and place it at the top of the stairs. I'll throw it in the box the knives came out of, chuck the whole lot into the van for taking to the charity shop tomorrow. Duncan's tools are all still in there, too. I've no need for tools. A lady like me doesn't work with tools. The lot of it needs to go. I don't want that missing knife coming back to haunt me.

I creep back to lie in Greg's arms. Maybe I could move to the next stage with Greg. Maybe I mean more to him than those others. He was so honest with me earlier about things most would keep secret. It's obvious he trusts me, until he says, half-asleep, 'Have you been checking my phone?' Then gives a snort and rolls over.

FIFTY-FIVE

RHIANNON

A FEELING of déjà vu flits over me, and I hesitate. The last time I opened a box of letters and journals, trouble reigned supreme.

On many levels, I know what I've done is evil. I killed a woman—nothing can change that fact. I'm unable to escape the feeling that I'm no longer a decent person. The stench of murder hangs around me, and I sense it always will.

'Come on, get on with it.' Preston shakes me out of my stupor, bringing my focus back to the job at hand.

I can force this lock, no bother.

With a screwdriver, I lever up the corners, moving all the way around, so it doesn't quite inch up as much as millimetre up. I've almost reached the point of frustration when it bursts open, the lid hitting the coffee table with a clunk.

We take in yellowed letters, still in their envelopes, the tops all jagged from the letter opener.

Ike grabs them and flips through, passing each one in turn onto me.

'Old letters. Very old letters.' Robyn sighs, as Ike takes a seat on the sofa.

On examination, I note that all are addressed to Winnie. Methodical as ever, I place them in order of date.

'There is nothing for me in here.' I hear Ike say.

'They're all from Patrick.' I mumble, reading through them in order, struggling with some passages due to the handwriting and language. I come to the obvious conclusion: they were in love. He adored Winifred, and it seems she felt the same early on.

'It's more to do with our investigation about the lady,' Preston suggests to Ike.

'Yes, all very interesting, I am sure.' Ike nods politely.

The letters leave a bittersweet taste. I've never known such devotion. I hear Preston chatting to Ike and Robyn, allowing me to carry on my reading.

'There was another Greg Holstead in our story. He was a lawyer, too. Related to your Mr. Greg,' Preston says.

Sadness creeps over me as I reach the last two letters. A similar melancholy to when I approach the final pages of a book I'm enjoying. I don't want the book to end, as my time in that universe and with those friends will finish forever.

'We think Patrick was dating the old bird who owned the house. Then he died in mysterious circumstances.'

Preston's chatter merges into the background as I delve into Patrick's words.

My Dear Winnie,

The past twelve months have been the happiest, the most irrationally happy of my life and have taught me more than one thing that I hope will be useful to me during the rest of that life.

I have learnt from you the joy of making small sacrifices for the benefit and happiness of others, and I have been taught the absurdity of relying on myself for triumphing over my shortcomings. This is all due to your example of Christian kindness. Let it be known I hold you, and will always hold you, in the highest of esteem. How very far I am yet from completely conquering my faults, and no one knows this so well
as I.

I did not receive your letter, my dearest, until after church time, which is the reason I greeted you as we have been accustomed. It will be to your knowledge, as you warned me in your letter, that the lawyer did indeed speak to me sternly about our increasing friendship—if that is how it could be named. Increasing affection would be a better term. No, indeed more than that. I love you deeply, fervently, and, oh, how happy should I be if I could only hope that my love was returned, although it seems it cannot be, due to other's opinions and concerns.

I will agree, as you wish, that we do not continue any courtship. I understand this is as you fear for me regarding the lawyer. I suppose you have changed your mind about going walking with me next Sunday, too. I cannot imagine having no chance of seeing you again, apart from across the kirk. It will make me the most wretched of men.

Please give my love to Eleanora. Goodnight my love. May God bless you.

Ever yours,
Patrick

I jump back into the present with Preston addressing me personally. 'You all right there, Rhiannon?'

'Yeah, yeah. He really loved her. There's word in here that a lawyer fella didn't want them together and had warned him off.'

'Gregory!'

'Indeed.'

Preston returns to speak to Ike and Robyn, allowing me to read the last letter. I take a breath, eking out the moment that must end. My heart races, and my pace increases. I'm not savouring every word, as I anticipated, but guzzling them, eager to discover what happened.

My dear Winnie,
I promised myself not to write again, after being warned not to spend time with you. But I want you to know that you are on my mind always.

I have your characterisation in front of me this very evening, so that I may gaze at you and speak with you at the same time.

What a stern face it wears, that composition, but nobody knows better than I how soon the face that inspired it can break into a smile. Indeed, I have waited almost every second to see a smile on the face in the portrait when I look at it.

This time last week, Lassie, I had a chance to remind myself of a pleasant evening spent down The Grove with you. It is pleasant to reflect on it.

The possession of your portrait, dear Winifred, makes me muse on something we have tacitly agreed not to write about.

Contemplating you has oftentimes—and I pray will again—helped me. Being able to see your visage, day to day, as I now can, for the greater part, would be better still.

I presume you have been sitting alone this evening, as have I. Why did I not impress on you to pay me a visit here, instead of going to The Grand House? The lawyer might not realise, and although it may not be possible, still I yearn.

Perhaps, as I have often heard that lassie with the earnest face say, 'It is all for the best, after all. Depend upon it, Patrick.'

But it is late. I must bid you goodnight and place your likeness out of sight and you out of mind, unless you are present in my dreams. Still, I can see you by daylight at the kirk, and ponder, without anyone knowing, what I might in bed.

Please give my love to Eleanora.
Goodnight, my love. May God bless you.

Ever yours,
Patrick

'Anything else in there, Rhiannon?'

'He took the painting as a memento and was struggling to stay away from her.'

'So, you think Gregory bumped him off, as he wouldn't be told!'

I glance at Ike's dejected face and announce, 'We have an envelope from The Grand House.'

Ike jumps forward. Preston must have nearly sent him to sleep.

'Oh yeah! We nicked it from the safe,' Preston adds with a smile to Ike.

'You got in the safe? I tried it, but I couldn't get the numbers.'

'That explains the books on the floor and the one's stacked up.'

'Oh no, not me. I left it very neat. Where is it? What does it say?'

'We didn't open it. It's at our flat.'

Within seconds, we are hot on Ike's heels out the door, leaving Robyn's door wide to the wall.

FIFTY-SIX
LYSSA

'ARE you going to the funeral on Tuesday?' Debbie has parked herself by Greg. She could do better by serving customers instead; we've been waiting for our coffees for quite some time.

I don't see Preston, and Rough is running around sweating buckets. *Sweaty staff is never a good advert. Honestly, I don't know why we keep coming to Debbie's café.*

'Yes,' Greg answers her.

Take a hint Debbie and get lost

'It will be a big turnout. Did you know him, Greg?'

'Yes, indeed, Fraser and I were old pals.'

'Isn't it awful how they've not caught anyone for it.' I chip in.

She looks me up and down. *It's like she's forgotten I'm here!*

'Well, actually, they might,' she says. 'You know the police were at my block the other night ...'

Greg raises his head and fixes Debbie in his sights.

'Um, so ... I don't know *exactly* what they were there for.' She flicks her hair behind her ear.

I flinch. *Louise? For the poison pen letters, obviously?* I run my fingers through my hair and accidentally knock over the milk with my pashmina fringe. 'Oh God. Sorry.'

'Lyssa!' Greg scolds.

I figure it is a positive that Debbie might actually have to lift a cloth, or leave to clean up, but no, she does not move.

'Roug—Julie!' She screams at the top of her voice, and then, back to a half whisper for us, adds, 'Well, Mr. Ross was in with Aunt Mary that night. You remember they are on the bottom floor? He saw the cop car at the door and gave himself up.'

'For what?' I ask.

'What we were talking about—the hit-and-run.' Her voice is so low now we're almost lip reading. 'He was out that night with Aunt Mary. He drove home late alone, and his eyesight isn't so good. He reckoned he must have knocked him down and not even noticed. As soon the cops were done upstairs, they were in at Auntie's flat interviewing him.'

I flick my gaze to Greg, hoping to catch any reaction, but I spot nothing discernible. 'They took him down the cop station. Apparently, he'd been fretting about it since he saw the report in the paper. Auntie is distraught. So is he, he wouldn't have meant it, you know?'

'Oh, for God's sake. It's a tragedy all round. Poor Fraser, though. You knew him so well, Greg, didn't you?' I say, staring at Debbie as I reach over to squeeze Greg's hand, pointing out to her that I know him best.

'Went on holiday a few times with the boys. Golfing buddies really. With Duncan, et al.'

I don't recall these holidays, and I cringe. More of Duncan's lies, and the fact that Greg was in on it causes my hand to recoil. I always thought he was working when he was not at home, not gallivanting with these chaps.

'Penny for your thoughts, Lyssa?' Debbie questions. My distaste must have shown on my face—another side effect of not getting my regular Botox.

'Sorry, I was just thinking that I need to go. I've another course to get to. I can't hang around here all day.' I leave the café in a rush, only pausing to look back at Debbie and Greg, all cosy in the window.

FIFTY-SEVEN

RHIANNON

'CHOICE ONE: Last chance to stick it under Lyssa's door,' announces Preston behaving like an American game show host and waving the envelope in my face. I try to snatch it, but he whips it away.

'Choice two: bin it. Or choice three: open it now. The decision is yours ...' He cackles.

'Open now,' interjects Ike, which snaps Preston back to his real-life persona.

'Good.' Preston rips it open and unfolds the top paper inside. 'Last Will and Testament. It's Duncan's will. Blah, blah, blah. I don't understand all that speak.'

'I do. Give it to me. I'll read it for you.' I grab it off him at last.

'Ooh, check the clever accountant.'

I stand to read it, as if giving a speech. 'Let me know if you wish to raise any questions or comments.' I snip.

'Oh, we will. Don't you worry.' Preston crosses his legs, in audience mode. Ike joins him.

'SINGLE LAST WILL AND TESTAMENT

'I, Mr. Duncan Whatmore of The Grand House,
Inveresk, Scotland, HEREBY REVOKE all former
Wills and testamentary dispositions made by
me AND DECLARE this to be my last Will.
'One: I APPOINT my trusted friend and
solicitor, Gregory Holstead, of Bridge
Street, Musselburgh, Scotland, to be the
Executor and Trustee of this, my Will.'

'Gee whizz, that guy gets everywhere.'
'We knew that anyway.'
'He's the main bloody character in everything.'

'… Provided that there should be at all
times one (1) Executor and Trustee of this,
my Will, so that in the event that my above-
named Executor and Trustee shall have pre-
deceased me or shall survive me but die
before the trusts hereof shall have
terminated or shall be unable or unwilling
to act or to continue to act, I appoint, in
the following order of priority, such one of
the persons hereinafter named as shall not
already be acting and as shall be able and
willing to act to fill the vacancy so
created, namely, my friend, Robert Ritchie,
of The Gardens, Musselburgh, Scotland.'

I stop myself from flinching at Rob's name in print. My only lover of
the last few years sits in prison, doing time for a murder I committed.
I did feel for him, I'm sure. It hurt me when he left, so I must have felt

something. How evil—to do what I did to someone I loved. I catch
Preston looking at me in silence, so I un-grit my teeth and carry on.

> '… And my friend Fraser McIntyre, of 4
> Woodside, Musselburgh. In this Will, the
> expression "my Trustees" means (as the
> context requires) those of my Executors who
> obtained probate and the Trustees for the
> time being of any trust arising under this
> Will.'

'Oh yeah, Fraser McIntyre. Bless his soul. I used to meet him on the
racecourse when I walked the dogs.'

> 'Two: My Trustees shall hold the remainder
> of my estate in trust for sale on the
> following terms: To pay debts and funeral
> and testamentary expenses. To pay
> inheritance tax in respect of property
> passing under the Will. To pay, transfer,
> and assign the residue of my estate to my
> wife, Alyssa Whatmore, for her use
> absolutely.'

'I BEG YOUR PARDON?' Preston butts in.
   'Ah, it is for Alyssa as Kwai Tan was told,' Ike utters.
   I freeze. 'Lyssa.' My breath catches in my throat. I manage to
squeak, 'Yes, Lyssa.' I repeat the last line again, enunciating every
syllable.

> 'To pay, transfer, and assign the residue of
> my estate to my wife, Alyssa Whatmore, for
> her use absolutely.'

I stare at Preston, who says, 'There must be more—'
'—I'll rattle through the rest,' I cut him off.

> 'Three: To my children, Jack and Carol, I
> leave the sum of 150,000 pounds. Four:
> Intentional Exclusion. I have deliberately
> excluded my ex-wife Stella from this, my
> Will, and it is my intention that the said
> should receive no part of my Estate for
> reasons given in a letter to my executors.

I take a breath in before I read out loud the next part.

> 'Five: To Kwai Tan, Geylang, Singapore, I
> leave 250,000 pounds.

'Ah, this is not what was told to Kwai Tan,' Ike pipes up.
'Or Lyssa ...!' adds Preston.
I continue.

> 'Distribution of the Residue. My Trustees
> shall hold the residue of my Estate to pay
> thereout all my debts, legacies, funeral and
> testamentary expenses and to any trusts
> declared earlier and subject thereto hold
> the remaining funds absolutely.'

I speak faster. 'There's more. I'll read the last bit quickly.

> 'Six: Funeral Wishes. I desire that my body
> be buried in Inveresk Cemetery.'

'Didnae happen,' Preston butts in, and Ike nods.
'Where is he, then? In Singapore?'

'Yes. It was arranged, but not by Kwai Tan. Mr. Greg told us it was Mrs. Lyssa wanted this.'

'What the hell! It's all the opposite of what happened.' Preston squeals.

'For both of them,' I add.

I scan it again, in case I misread it. My mouth feels dry. Preston grabs the will and reads out the last part.

```
'The Testimonium and Attestation SIGNED by
Duncan Whatmore on the day of 20th May 2022.
Signature of Testator: D Whatmore
SIGNED by the testator in our presence and
attested by us in the presence of the
Testator and each other
Witness number 1 Signature: K. Ritchie
Full Name: Kimberley Ritchie
Address: The Gardens, Musselburgh, Scotland
Occupation: Receptionist/Manager
```

'Ha! Good old Kim!' Preston blusters. I fold my arms in a huff at her name. Preston continues.

```
'Witness number 2 Signature F McIntyre. Full
name: Fraser McIntyre.
Address: 4 Woodside, Musselburgh Scotland.
Occupation: Surveyor.
```

'The End!' I sit down, feeling as if my legs might stop working as I remember what happened to Kim.

'This is a nightmare. We've uncovered a nightmare.'

'Too right, Rhiannon. You can say that until the cows come home to roost.'

FIFTY-EIGHT

LYSSA

'I SUIT BLACK. It shouldn't suit me with my colouring,' I announce out loud, posing in the mirror.

'What's that?' Greg calls from the hall and then enters the room.

'I said: I suit black.'

'You do. You'd look beautiful, even in a bin bag.' He kisses my cheek and I smile.

'What? A black one?'

He pulls his black tie off and lounges on the bed, yawning.

'Yes, a black one. Any one. Thank God that's over. I hate funerals. What a waste of a day.'

'And tea in the manky old hall at the Imperial, too. Ugh, I think those sandwiches had been left lying there all morning,' I add.

'I'll go shower.' He says, hauling himself up again.

'I'll go in after you,' I reply.

He takes his phone. He's being doing that more and more. Lately, I haven't had a chance to check his messages. I'm over doing so anyway. It's only caused trouble.

We swap places in the bathroom. Greg leaves the shower running for me. He is so kind at times.

The room steams up, so I don't notice his phone right in the middle of the floor, until I kick it accidentally. I pick it up. *Hello, old friend.*

Will I? Well, of course. It would be rude not to, and I've done it so many times before, it would hardly matter.

I hold it to my chest and say a quick prayer before opening it up. *Please let there be nothing.* After swiping the screen, a new name floors me.

Kwai Tan: Thank you so much, Mr. Greg sir.

No problem

Is the house nearly sold?

It could be a week or even months. Years, for this type of property, would not be out of the question. There is some legal work to arrange even after a sale is agreed.

Thank you for my son and me.

AND NOTHING ELSE. I feel heavy. So much has happened this year. If you'd told me this before, I would have said you were mad.

There's nothing else suspicious. In fact, there are no other messages at all. It's as if no-one else has messaged him since the last time I checked. Louise has disappeared altogether. He's obviously blocked her and deleted her contact. She must be in the 'business only' section of his life. I feel relieved. This worst of this turmoil must be over.

I've been silly and jealous. I've taken things too far. No more will

I look at his phone. There's no need. I head to bed, but Greg is already unconscious.

Just when I feel settled, even sleepy, my phone buzzes.

A message from Debbie appears.

Debbie: **Lyssa, we really need to talk.**

I know I won't sleep now!

FIFTY-NINE

RHIANNON

I GRIND my teeth at the name: Kimberley Ritchie. My dentist tells me my masseter muscle is working overtime. How did Kim come to be one of the witnesses to the will? I'd dealt with her in the most final of manners. Due to my actions, she would never tell her side of this story.

'So, this will leaves everything mainly to Lyssa.'

'And some to Kwai Tan,' Ike jumps in. 'Not all, like I hoping.'

'Maybe he made a new one after this?' I suggest, trying to calm myself down.

'Okay. Sure, maybe. Apart from that both women have been told different stories. Each told the other gets the money.' Preston looks unconvinced.

'And this is recent,' I continue, after checking the dates again.

'We must do something about this, and I don't mean sticking it under Lyssa's door and running away. Greg is the executor. Should we deliver it to him?' I simper the last words, already knowing that is out of the question.

'Are you kidding me? You aren't getting this!' Preston stamps his foot melodramatically. 'He's *behind* this, for sure. I can read him like the back of my book!'

'He is a bad man,' Ike adds with a nod.

'He'll be keeping the house for himself, and any money. I've a feeling—' Preston begins.

'—Not good enough, chaps,' I interrupt. 'Gut feelings don't count for much legally. Think about it logically.'

Ike sits between the now-standing Preston and me, as if watching a tennis match while we bat our ideas back and forth.

'Righty-ho, Miss Logic. He's been looking for this, I tell you. He knows it exists, and it contradicts the two he fabricated—the one that lets him sell the house and be in charge of the proceeds. That's why he's been hanging around Lyssa, helping her unpack, turning up when she isn't in. That's why the office was turned upside down in the old house. He's on the hunt for this very document!'

Preston holds the will up to the light, and we stare at it as if it were the Holy Grail. He continues, 'What if he had something to do with Duncan's death, too? He is capable, just like his great grandfather. He's already done Lyssa and Kwai Tan out of the house and money, what if he is also a murderer, if you follow where I'm coming from.'

'Duncan might have had a load of debts,' I counter. 'The house might have needed sold so maybe there would be little left for the ladies afterwards. That's still an option.'

'Clutching at hairs there, Rhiannon.'

'It needs ruling out.'

'Come on. It's sticking out like a sore leg what actually happened here.'

'Hell. Do you really think he'd be capable of murder? Is it just not an opportunity he has seen?' I lean on the counter, my head in my hands. I know fine well, of all people, that anyone could be capable of murder.

Ike looks confused, but Preston begins again. 'Kim's well gone.

Think about it. Fraser, the single living witness to the true will, is dead now, too. Greg's more than a dodgy dealer. He's dangerous!'

'Killed by a green car,' I murmur my thoughts out loud, and I can't stop myself from scanning Ike up and down.

'Louise, Greg's other woman also drives a green car.' Ike submits in answer.

Preston looks even more convinced. 'He'll be behind it. I tell you, I knew that guy was out to butter his own parsnips the whole time.'

'Parsnips?' Ike repeats, confused.

'Never mind, Ike.' I wave Preston off.

'We must trap him into a confession,' Preston announces. Ike seems to understand this more than any of the last ten minutes of two loud Scottish people shouting at each other.

'Preston, we have what Mr. Greg wants: the will. Get him to meet you. Tell him we know everything. I have a friend who could wire you up, so I can record the conversation,' Ike suggests.

'Okay, I'll do it.'

'You never struck me as a James Bond type, Preston,' I snip, curling my lip.

'Oh aye, Mish Moneypenny. Oh, I just thought of something, Rhiannon. We saw Greg there when we left The Grand House. Are you sure he saw us?'

'Probably.'

'Did you shut the safe?'

'I think so.'

'Okay, but even if he didn't clock us, Tony might have told him we were there. Greg knows we can't afford to buy that huge pile, even between us. Get on to Pound-shop Pierce, see what you can wheedle out of him.'

'Pardon?'

'Ask him on a date.'

'Oh, I can't. I'm too shy.'

'It's life or death, Rhiannon.' Preston begs. 'You have to do your part!'

'I'll text him,' I say gripping my phone so hard that my knuckles go white. I make no move to text.

'Give me that.' Preston grabs my phone and read outs as he types.

Hi Tony,
I hope you don't think I'm being forward
but would you like to catch up for a coffee?

He pauses. 'To put a kiss, or not? Oh, to hell. **x.** We need to lay the trap.'

'With me as the bait.' I fold my arms.

He stares at me. 'Mmm. You'll need a bit of work.'

'Thanks.' I purse my lips and straighten my top.

SIXTY

LYSSA

'WHY DID YOU HIT ON DEBBIE?' I blurt out. There's no way to dress this up.

Greg gives a rueful smile. He wears an expression of ...

What is that? Pity?

He tilts his head, with his lip out, as if mocking me for pouting about a silly little thing like that.

'I didn't, darling! She made it up. She's not a good friend to you. Obviously, she's just jealous, or maybe she wants me for herself?' He holds me by my shoulders and stares at me straight on.

I scan his face. His ability to lie is incredible. I note no signs of deception. I almost believe him. Until I shake out of his hypnotic gaze.

Turning to the side, I say, 'She wouldn't lie. I believe her.' I glance back to view his reaction. Greg's face contorts in front of me. He resets.

Was this an attempt to break up our friendship? I'd heard of men like this, who isolate women from their immediate friends and family. His reply surprises me.

'Okay, I'll be honest. I did. It was a moment of madness.' His head drops down for this statement. He possessed a lot more confidence in the outright lie.

'She was flirting with me, though.' He raises his head again. She is not innocent in all this. She led me on.'

'Why did you lie?'

'Pardon?'

'Why did you lie that you hadn't done it?'

He coughs a laugh. 'Because I don't want to lose you.' He reaches over to touch my hand. 'I did it for you.'

My reaction clearly surprises him. I have always been so compliant; he probably assumed I'd melt.

'I can't deal with this. I can't trust you!'

His face morphs into another expression. He is losing control.

'We are done, you have to go.'

His hands drop to his side in exasperation. He laughs, more openly this time, in disbelief. 'You, *you* are finishing with me? Are you joking?'

'I can't tolerate that. It's an ultimate betrayal. Did you not think there would be consequences if you slept with my best friend?'

'I didn't sleep with her.'

'You tried to.'

'I can't believe this.' He shakes his head.

'What did you expect?'

'What did I expect? What did *you* expect, Lyssa?' He contorts my name into a hiss.

'What?' *This is taking an unexpected turn.*

'Do you not imagine I'd rather her than you. I mean, look at the difference between you. She has curves in all the right places.'

'But all that you said to me. You said I was gorgeous.'

'Honestly, are you that stupid? I said those things to get you into bed.'

I take a breath, and with some confidence say, 'If I'm so disgusting, why would you bother?'

He doesn't answer. He smirks, lying across the bed, his head balanced on his hand.

'And, frankly, if that is how you feel about me, I feel better about my decision to finish with you. You obviously don't care for me at all.'

He smiles in silence. He has the upper hand somehow, as I am flapping around looking for some sense in this conversation.

'Hold on, you said you didn't want to lose me a matter of minutes ago,' I point right at him. My stomach is turning over. None of his behaviour makes any sense. All the tension and stress of the last little while is coming out. I can't keep it all in anymore.

Greg lifts himself up to standing, takes me by the shoulders, and pushes me down on the bed. He paces, as if in a courtroom, making a damning final summing up.

So?' He rocks on his feet, his hand on his chin. 'Would you not think there could be another reason. I mean, what is the attraction? In your mind ... why would I want you?'

'I'm beautiful. I dress well. I'm sophisticated. Erm, my personality.'

'Laughable. Yeah, okay. Have a wee ponder about why penniless me would want a woman with money?'

'You're penniless? You are here for money?'

'Temporarily. But don't judge me. Women behave like this all the time.'

'Prostitutes perhaps. So, you're a gigolo?' I spit.

His face falls. He is not laughing now. 'That's not how this goes, Lyssa. No, what happened, dear,' he says, 'was that I lured you into loving me with sex and lies, and I rightly want something in return. Your substantial insurance windfall is due very soon. Poor Alyssa is down to her last 450K! Boo hoo!' His lips curl in a mock cry. 'You women are so easy to take in. So stupid as to believe men could fall in love with your old saggy, run-through bodies. All of you get old and past it. You surely know only youthful women are of any real value to men of my stature.' His head tilts to the side, his half-smile is back.

I grip the bed cover.

'Do you not think I'd rather be seen with, and screw, a hot twenty-year-old. It's nature—biology, if you like—you can't fight it. You are nubile women but for a short while, and then you go off.' He looks around and laughs in disbelief with his arms wide. 'Then I'm chastised when I'm kind enough to overlook that and consider your ... other assets ... as I'm a little short right now.'

'Debbie isn't young!' I bite.

'Neither of you are high-value women,' he snaps. She has the allure of some cash about her, like you. She is ... just another easy option. As soon as you old gals realise your worth and position in these arrangements, the better. I get some money. You get the status of being seen with me and not being a sad old cat lady. Everything is a trade-off.'

I can barely breathe as he stands over me. I push past him and stumble over to the sideboard, leaning on it with my back to him.

'Are you finished?' I force out.

I hear him snort. 'Yeah, I'm finished. Finished with you, you worn out old hag.' He pauses. 'But I'm not a bad guy. I might forgive your little outburst. Call me when you come to your senses and work out this is the best you can ever get.'

I turn to see him gone and slump onto the bed.

SIXTY-ONE

RHIANNON

I CANNOT BELIEVE I am doing this. I mean, I am excited to meet Tony, but my stomach keeps turning over and over.

I promised Preston and Ike I'd ask about Greg, but how I'll fulfil that task without sounding suspicious, I'm not sure. This scenario all seems so far-fetched. I struggle to wrap my head around how Greg would chance carrying this plan out. Surely, he risks discovery—by the authorities, by the foreign office, or by the law society. People uncover wrongdoings that leave traces and paper trails. If all the money ended up in Greg's account, wouldn't questions be asked?

The debts Duncan had must be a better explanation. As for the question of murder, how could Greg have killed Duncan when he died in Singapore?

I ball my hands into fists within my jacket pockets. I'm not wearing my hoodie today. I'm dressing to impress. I sport a cross-over bag, instead of my rucksack. And Preston insisted I wear heels, although I can hardly walk in them. Since lockdown, I'm a trainer's girl. He straightened my frizz of hair and even made me put make-up on. I feel conspicuous, standing on the High Street outside Debbie's, although no one cares.

I kick a stone from the path to the road. I'm far too early, as usual. I boot another stone and concentrate on it rolling away into the gutter. I am so fixated on it that I don't notice Tony until I smell his aftershave.

I step back. I'm not accustomed to having men near me. Not since Rob. I stop breathing.

'You wanted to see me?' He grins.

I grin back. His smile is infectious. I'm ruminating, not speaking; staring, not conversing. I snap myself out of my hypnosis to say, 'Yes, yes, I thought I might.'

'I like it. A woman who knows what she wants! And would madam wish a cup of tea?' He opens the door.

We enter Debbie's unromantic first-date setting. I feel safe not going somewhere fancy and out of my comfort zone, much to Preston's chagrin.

'So, tell me about yourself,' Tony begins.

'Oh, not much to tell. I'm an accountant. Quite boring, I suppose. I like long walks.' *God, I sound boring.* 'Hiking.'

'I walked a lot during lockdown. Sure clears the mind.' He is kind enough not to roll his eyes at my dullness. I remind myself that I must divert the conversation to Greg.

'So, you know Greg? He is dating my friend.'

'Is he now?' Tony rocks back, letting his arms spread wide. 'I did wonder if he would have been after a catch like you.' He leans forwards. 'How has no one snapped you up? Greg likes the ladies, that's for sure. Has a good deal of success with them.'

He seems impressed. I'm not and cross my legs.

'Ah, sure. He isn't one to want to be tied down,' Tony adds. 'You know him well?'

'In passing (on the stair!) but he seems very nice,' I drop in, as Rough arrives with our drinks.

'Ah, thank you, young lady,' he says to her. I giggle, and Rough flicks her hair in appreciation at the compliment.

'Nice, nice, nice.' Tony adds a lot of sugar to his tea. I don't imagine he needs the energy, as his movements are rapid and many.

'I don't know whether I would describe Greg as nice. Driven, yes. Confident, for sure.'

'Arrogant?' I suggest cowering behind my teacup.

'A-ha! That's probably a better word!' He laughs, but then checks himself. 'No, no. I don't mean to speak ill of him. I do admire him, in a way, for his risk taking, his ruthlessness in business.'

'Oh yeah?'

'Something I am lacking. I'm more of a sentimental type. I believe if you do a good turn, it comes back to you, you understand?' I agree with a nod, although I hope karma is not an exact science.

'It does get him into trouble sometimes. He has problems, too, with the gambling, but I probably shouldn't say too much about that. Now, do you like travel?'

'I've been a few places in Europe and America. I'd like to travel more. How about you?'

'I love a change of scene. It gives a different perspective when you realise how big the world is and see life carrying on elsewhere for other people.'

I watch his lips move and his eyes twinkle. *Boy, I am hooked.* 'Been anywhere recently?' I say, to break up my gawping.

'A boys' trip to London. Greg was there.'

Now I perk up. I return to my mission. 'A good time?'

'Yeah, but Greg ... There was one incident. He takes a good bit to drink. I swear he nearly killed the tube worker who told him he was using the wrong escalator. I thought he was going to strangle him. We dragged him away. He's quite a temper on him.'

'So, you know each other well enough to go on holiday together, then?'

'Ach, there were a group of us. Mainly from Greg's gang. They often meet up abroad, Madrid one time, Dubai, Singapore. Fraser McIntyre was one of them. He's dead now, of course. God rest his soul. And Duncan Whatmore—dead now, too—he was another.'

'You knew Duncan?'

'Yeah, he was a great guy.'

'I was at school with Lyssa,' I tell him.

'You don't look old enough.' He winks.

What a lie.

'Duncan was a fine chap. You'd know, if you were close to his wife. He was very good with money. A great believer in having no debt. He didn't believe folk needed a credit score. Like we'd all been fed that over the years, and we'd collectively believed it. He was also known as a tight wad.' He laughs.

I sigh.

'Tell me more about your boys' trips?' I probe.

'It wasn't just trips. I'm on the sidelines, as a friend of a friend. Greg runs this group—Men's Men, he calls it. Like a training programme, almost, to teach men how to exist as a man in this modern world. He had this idea it could be really big.'

'Right.' I mumble. I'm too busy taking in the Singapore mention and Duncan's lack of debt to concentrate properly, until he adds, 'He had rules, like men should be masculine and women feminine.'

I look up from my tea. My eyebrows feel like they are hitting my hairline. I pull them down to a less-exciting position. 'What other rules?'

'Erm, like ... to succeed, it is okay to lie.'

'What?'

'Ah, that sounds bad, but it's like Greg says: everyone has the right to lie. The people you are lying to have a right to lie, too, so just make sure you are better at it.'

I contemplate all the lies I've told in the past, including my major one involving a strangulation in the lagoons. I can't feel outraged for hypocritical reasons.

'This is for business, you s-see,' he stutters.

'Go on, I understand.'

'Yes, in business, not in relationships.' His hand comes across the table to touch mine. I flush at the relationship idea.

'Go on.'

'Greg teaches there are basically three parts to make a lie work. One: tell the person what they want to hear. Two: tell something close to the truth. Three: look the person in the eye and say it with the appropriate emotion.'

I nod.

'In addition, he suggests leading the susceptible down a lot of the wrong tracks, and it's okay to accuse them of being terrible and unhelpful, subtly, whenever you can, to sort of undermine their confidence.'

'Negging?' I suggest.

'Negging?'

'Saying negative things to people to make them doubt themselves. Then, all of a sudden, they think less of themselves, they like you more, and they want to please you more.'

'Yeah. When I hear you say it, it doesn't come across the way Greg puts it. But that seems about right.' His brow furrows.

'Good God.' I can't keep it in.

'Oh, I struggle with it, too. I'm not that great at it. Greg says I'm too much of an open book. Talking of open, I need to share something with you.' He looks at me long and hard.

'Oh?'

'I must visit the gents! Ha! Got you!' He springs up and dashes away.

I still like Irish. His heart seems in the right place, but Greg's influence, and all this alpha male crap, is off-putting. I take the opportunity to Text Preston.

I agree with you now. Tony told me Greg was in Singapore with Duncan one time. Maybe Duncan's last time. Also Duncan never had any debts. He was well known for it.

**I'm going to meet Greg
right now!**

What now?
Where? When?

**I phoned him at his
Office. All I said was
I know everything**

What??? Right now?

**He said 'Meet me at the
allocated time and place.
8 pm Haddington.'**

Why Haddington?

His idea!

SHIT! *That's in an hour.*

Tony appears at my side.

'I need to go, Tony. An emergency!' I stand and stuff my phone into my bag. In a hurried moment of madness, I grab his face and kiss him.

'Wow ... I'll call you!' I hear him say, as I dash out the door.

SIXTY-TWO

LYSSA

I CAN'T GET Greg and all he said out of my head. I'm trying to make sense of the last months, but my head hurts. I sit at the computer and check Greg's socials. I do the same for Louise, Karina and Robyn. I see nothing new.

I am torturing myself.

Greg's flat in Leith pops into my head. I try the sites on the Internet where you find the cost of the properties. I find it was bought in 2009 for 145,000 pounds. *What is the point of this?* I Google its address, on the off chance I can view the particulars of when he bought it or see inside it—just to make sure it exists, and I didn't imagine this whole experience. Top of the search, I see:

Commercial Street, Leith—Flats for Rent
Entire rental unit for £85 per night. A bright, stylishly modern third-floor, one-bedroom apartment in a warehouse conversion in Leith. Includes private parking.

I know it includes private parking. We parked there. It's a holiday rental!

Where does he live, then? I scan the photos. Everything is as I remember it, down to the duvet cover. I think of Rhiannon's search advice months ago. I pay twenty pounds to the land registry to find the owner. The email with the information arrives soon after:

Owners: Gregory Holstead and Louise Lacey

What the hell is going on with these two?
I text him:

**Hey honey, can
you forgive me xx**

> **Ha! Can't stay away,
> huh? x**

**Come over. We can talk. I know
I upset you and we both said things
we didn't mean x**

> **You women are so easy to predict.
> Once you've had a taste
> of a top-dog man, you can't
> get enough. It's the natural order.
> It's good you are learning!**

Can you come over? x

> **I can't. I've business tonight**

The phone pings again. Is it him? No, it's a message from Debbie: a voice note.

I hit play.

'Tonight's drama, Lyssa. Mr. Ross is off the hook. Never guess what. He'd got the dates muddled up. He and Auntie were in Callander on a bus tour that night. He remembered, but not before the police had gone to the effort of checking his car and finding not a mark.'

Who cares!

I look out the window over to Greg's office. The dim back light is on. It is 7.30pm and getting dark. I flinch as I see the light go off. Some business he is doing. I watch Greg leave and head to his parked car. Where is he going now? More importantly, *who* is he going *to* now?

I grab my pashmina and throw my keys and phone in to my Orla Keily bag. I have to drive this stupid van, with all the charity shop boxes and tools in the back. It's so conspicuous, but I hope that it looks like a regular work van from the front.

I turn out of the car park in time to see Greg at the traffic lights. I hold back, hoping I don't lose him. I halt at the lights, five cars behind him, but see him drive over the bridge, only to get stopped at the next set of lights. They always take ages, so I'm not worried.

That bloody green car spins out of Eskside, let out by the car two in front of me while I am still static. *Louise!* Is she in pursuit, like me? Or meeting him in a secret location? *God knows what's going on.*

I drive on to catch up with them at the lights. Looking left toward bland Karina's block, I see her exit the doorway, swinging her car keys. *Where is she going now?*

Greg and Louise both turn into the High Street. I follow. And then I spot Robyn and her massive behind getting into a taxi. And there Debbie is, shutting up shop for the night, pulling the shutters down on the café.

I'm so mad at Greg. He goes through life putting on a different face for everyone, lying all the time so people will like him and do what he says. He charms them all, but who is the real Greg? I bet he doesn't even know the authentic version. It's like he doesn't exist at all, floating about like a ghost or a figment of his own imagination.

On and on, I follow them, deep into the countryside. Where we will end up, I do not know, but I'm not letting go now.

SIXTY-THREE

RHIANNON

SHIT, *shit, shit! Hurry up!* I scold myself while waiting for the fuel to fill the tank. There's no way I can travel all the way to Haddington with nothing in the tank. What the hell was Preston thinking, meeting him tonight? He could have waited till I was free. I text him again:

**Where about in Haddington
for the millionth time?**

> **I'm here now.
> Mad early like you
> always are.
> He isn't here yet.**

**Coordinates now! Go on your 'What three words
app' I gave you. The one that works out where
you are and gives you three words that relate to**

it. And tell me the words that relate to your position.

> **Okay, it's coming out as
> nearly. decent. thigh.
> Ha-ha that's funnee**

I curse myself for not filling up yesterday. The self-service card machine by the pump isn't working. And, of course, two other folks beat me to the cashier. In front of me are 'Motorbike guy' and 'Guy who came into the garage after me'—he only put a fiver's worth of petrol in, ensuring his current queue position. But he's grabbed as many snacks as he can hold on his way to the counter, being careful not to let me overtake him. He dithers about choosing which cigarettes he wants. Oh, and now a scratch card, too. At last, his transaction finishes. I tap and go.

The woman in front of me is still parked in position. I fasten my seatbelt. *Here she comes now, back from the trash.* She has been tidying out her car, blocking the way!

I start up the Sat Nav again for Haddington centre. It said eighteen minutes away when I picked up the car at the flats, but I've used ten minutes getting fuel. I'm further away from Haddington than where I started. I glance up. *Come on Lady. Sit down, seatbelt and drive. Jesus H … Is she fixing her hair and makeup?*

I stick my head out the window and pump the horn 'Yeah, you look fantastic!' I yell. 'Let's go!'

Finally, she moves. I nearly knock the guy who served me over, as he rushes out of the shop for some reason, but at last I'm on my way.

I seem to hit every traffic light through Musselburgh, but I tear on up to join the A1, where flowers lie wilting in memory of Fraser McIntyre.

I'm making decent time now. I park at the Corn Exchange and fire up the app on my phone. The 'what three words' reference turns out to be a ten-minute walk through some houses to the river. It schedules my arrival for five minutes past. I march on, as fast as I am able to in these shoes, and soon find myself on a path obscured by trees. 8pm. Preston should be here now. As I approach my destination, I hear voices and put my phone on silent. I scan the area, viewing the back of their heads, where they sit on a bench.

What a wonderful place for a confrontation with a sociopath—a deserted riverside walkway.

SIXTY-FOUR

RHIANNON

'IT'S time to step up to the plate and lay your cards on the table, mister,' Preston announces, standing up from the bench, his hands on his hips.

'What?' Greg shakes his head and remains seated. I can only see his back.

'I know everything.'

'So you said. Okay, you can stop this now. I don't know what you think you know. But you are wrong.' Greg crosses his legs and spreads his arm over the backrest.

'You understand fine what I mean.'

'How about you tell me your theory, and I'll explain how this is all in your imagination.'

'You faked Duncan's will, for a start.'

Greg's arm drops. 'And you can't prove that, so ... conversation over.' He stands and starts to walk away.

'Oh no. I can. I have the original will.'

Greg spins, giving me a good view of his face. His eyes narrow, and I lean back against a tree to listen.

'No, you don't. I hunted up and down for that.'

'I have it.'

'You don't. Where did you get it?' Greg spits.

'In the big house, in a safe.'

'Shit.'

'In your grandfather's house.'

'Yeah, my grandfather's house. Is that why you and Plain Jane were there?'

I dare peep out again, watching Greg fold his arms smugly.

'How did he lose it?'

'Pardon?'

'How did he lose the house?'

'He gambled it away. How have you any information about my grandfather? Did Lyssa tell you this?'

'Like taking a gamble, do you? Your great-great-great grandfather did a murder, too!'

'What on Earth are you on about? What murder?'

'And you. You're one, too!'

'I'm one what?'

'A murderer.'

Greg unfolds his arms and paces like a barrister in a film. Pointing at Preston's face, he spits through his teeth, 'No one is going to believe a convict. You were involved in a murder yourself already.'

'Takes one to smell one.'

'Ah, but you're not a murderer, Preston. You were aiding and abetting, merely hiding a body in a wheelie bin—badly, I might add.' Greg laughs.

'No, I slit that bastard's throat. I don't mind you knowing that Angela took the hit for it.

'Really, Preston? You've gone up in my estimation. However, you still did the time. The difference between you and me, Preston, is that I'm more efficient at murder than you.'

'The point is that you killed Fraser.'

Greg bites his lip for a second and tilts his head to the side. 'Fraser who?'

'McIntyre. The only living witness to the real will.'

'Boy oh boy, you have it all worked out, don't you? That wasn't me. An associate of mine. Indeed, all I had to do was a wee bit of paperwork and the family home was mine again. I've no love of the old place, but it seems fitting that it is providing me with my rightful lifestyle in the end.'

'And Duncan?'

'Ah, yeah. Now you *are* getting around to my dirty work. Poor Duncan's heart pills in his hotel drawer were gift. An easy swap for some ... more dramatic medicine. I popped back to Scotland for some business, and the next day, I let nature take its course. None of this can be proven—you do know that?' He grins.

'I've all the evidence, right here.' Preston withdraws the will from his jacket and brandishes it.

'Now, that was silly, wasn't it? Bringing the evidence with you. Thank you for that.' Greg shoves Preston, snatches the paperwork off him, and pockets it.

I sigh inwardly.

'What will you do with it?' Preston whimpers.

'It's going the very place my original copy is right now.' Greg points to a small boat by the water's edge. 'My copy is dissolved in the water. Disappeared into tiny pieces.'

Preston pauses. 'Lyssa said you owned a boat. That's yours?' He cackles. 'The way she talked about it, it was a yacht. That's a bloody rowboat, ya big bawheid.'

Greg's fists tighten. Preston stops laughing and launches himself at Greg, knocking him to the ground, where they grapple in the dirt.

My legs suddenly won't work. Frozen to the spot, I grip the bark behind me, too scared to move, watching as Greg sits astride Preston, his hands around my friend's neck.

Shit! I unstick myself from behind my tree and spring into action, careening over on my ankle and falling flat on my face on the path, ripping my clothes. The metallic taste of blood fills my mouth, and a raw, stinging feeling on my cheek and hands fills my eyes with tears.

Noticing me, Greg twists his head and groans. 'Not another idiot!'

I feel like a helpless heroine in a horror movie—the same ones I shout at for being stupid. Leaving Preston floundering and coughing, Greg grabs my leg and turns me onto my back. Greg's hands are around my neck now. I can't breathe. I flail helplessly, clutching his jacket, scratching my nails into his hands. A kaleidoscope pattern dances in front of my eyes.

Is this how Kim felt?

They say your life flashes before your eyes when you are about to die—not for me. All I see is all my regrets, all my mistakes, accompanied by the feeling that I deserved this. Karma has come for me.

Just as I resign myself to my fate, a black blur of movement flits behind Greg. My eyes close, but I hear a dull thump and feel Greg's grip release. I gulp air into my lungs like a starving woman imbibing food.

Greg falls with a thud to my right, his meaty arm across me. I eyeball his glazed eyes, and then push him away and scramble backward, scratching my palms on loose gravel to get away from his body. Looking up, I spy a shadowy figure standing over him in the twilight.

SIXTY-FIVE

RHIANNON

'LYSSA!' Preston cries from the riverbank.

I see her clearly now, leaning over Greg carrying ... *What is that? A crucifix!* I scramble over on my knees and haul myself up. *Stupid heels!* I knew I shouldn't have worn them. I grab Lyssa, who looks like she may topple over.

'He didn't repent,' she whimpers.

'Okay. Okay, sit down,' I choke out.

Preston continues to cough, too, but manages to add, 'Get the will.'

I pull it out of Greg's inside pocket and check on him. No pulse.

Now-kneeling, Lyssa is still gripping her crucifix.

'Where did you get that, Lyssa?'

'Tenerife.' She seems dazed. 'It's mine and Duncan's.'

'I mean, where did you get it in the forest?' I look around at our surroundings.

'From the van. My van. Angela's van. It was in the boxes. I left it in there to take to the charity shop with the knives.'

'Knives? You've a box of knives with you, too?'

'And power tools.' Her voice is a monotone.

'Right.'

'Greg has a spade, some rope and tarpaulin in his boot. He left it open. I'm parked next to his car.' She points along the path. 'I thought he was going to kill you, Preston. And you, Rhiannon. I heard what he said to you. I was listening. I didn't know he did all those things. He was a womaniser and after my money. He told me as much. But I needed to know more.' She scans the area. 'I don't know where Louise, Robyn and Karina are. Louise was there for a while, but she turned off to Prestonpans, and Greg came here on his own.'

'Louise?' I question.

'Who's Louise?' Preston asks.

'Louise, the Kiwi.'

I scan for anyone else lurking, like I was.

Ike appears out of nowhere.

'It's Louise's night for A.A.—Monday night.'

'Yes, it is,' murmurs Lyssa, 'but I saw a green car when I went back to the van.' She looks around for Louise again.

'Mine.'

'You're the baseball-cap man.'

Ike removes his hat and nods. 'Ike.'

'He's with us,' is the only explanation I give.

'I heard him talk about the will, and the bit about Fraser, and then Duncan. So, I went back to the van to fetch this.' She stares numbly at the crucifix, as if she's never seen it before and has no idea how it landed in her hand. 'I went back to get Jesus on the cross. He deserved it, didn't he?' Lyssa wails. 'It's blood debt, like Jesus Christ died for our sins. His blood paid for our sins. I can't go to jail.'

Preston throws me a quizzical look and his mouth gapes open.

I shake my head at him. 'Yes, he did deserve it. He was a bad man.' I put my arm around her. 'I'll help you.'

'We'll both help you,' adds Preston, pushing himself up. 'I've been here before. It's like diggie view.'

'Déjà vu,' I correct him.

'I cannot help with this situation. I cannot risk being involved in such things,' Ike states, both palms held up towards us.

'Are you going to tell the police?' Lyssa whimpers.

'Of course not,' Preston answers.

Ike stares at the ground.

'I think we're past that,' Preston adds. 'Kwai Tan gets money in the real will, too.'

'Whether I say anything or not,' Ike adds.

'Lyssa, promise him some money for keeping his trap shut,' Preston says.

'I promise you one hundred thousand pounds,' Lyssa announces.

'Fine. I will have nothing more to do with this. I speak with you in ten days.' Ike swiftly retrieves the recording wire from Preston. 'Remember, I have this.' He turns directly to Lyssa. 'I will be in touch.'

I watch him disappear, almost silently, into the darkness.

'You killed your brother, Preston. I can't believe it.' Lyssa glares at him.

'You can dismount your high horse right now, your ladyship,' Preston warns. 'You just clubbed someone to death with Our Lord and Saviour.'

'But Angela was innocent this whole time,' she moans.

'Let sleeping dogs lie doon, I tell you!' Preston hisses, pointing to the corpse.

Lyssa turns her head away to retch.

'How to dispose of the body?' I ask, and they both gawp at me.

I feel my lips tighten as I roll up my sleeves.

Neither of them says a thing.

Inspiration strikes. 'Tools, knives, rope, tarpaulin, and a spade, you say?'

SIXTY-SIX

LYSSA

'I NEVER REALISED DIGGING a grave would be so difficult. On television, they produce a perfect rectangular hole in minutes, with a neat pile of dirt next to it, ready for filling in—after they've checked for car headlights, passers-by and dog walkers, that is. I didn't reckon on this! Roots, stones and random things in the way! An old brick. A broken milk bottle. Things that make no sense in a field, unless someone else hid something around here ... another body maybe ...'

'More digging, less talking, Lyssa!' Rhiannon orders.

'Mind on and not break a nail,' snips Preston.

But I don't stop. I haven't stopped talking nearly the whole time. My mouth nervously runs away with me still.

'I haven't dug a grave before, but I suppose the main rule is not to dig so deep that the hole is taller than yourself, or else you might not escape either, right?'

'You're jabbering, Lyssa.'

We're almost finished. I lean against a tree and stare back to the walkway across the river. Preston and Rhiannon ferried Greg over on his boat and hauled him up the steep bank to the edge of this farmer's field, while I fetched the equipment.

'Why couldn't we have left him on the other side?' I ask.

'We won't encounter passers-by in the field. We were lucky to drag him over here, past these trees, without being seen.' Preston looks at Rhiannon, as if for confirmation. She nods.

'And if you think it's difficult to dig this soil, it would have been way worse over among the trees riverside, with all their roots,' Rhiannon adds.

I have a hundred questions. We whisper back and forth. 'Will the farmer not catch us?'

'Not at this time of night.'

'I don't understand why he needs to be naked?'

'Trust me, I'm on it. It's buying us time.'

'And why wrap him in the tarpaulin and rope?'

'Shush.'

'And also, why did you stab him, Rhiannon?'

'Again, I'm not going over it again.'

'Are we leaving the knife with him?'

'Yes. It's all our insurance policy. Gosh, I've never heard you talk so much, Lyssa!'

SIXTY-SEVEN

RHIANNON

LYSSA FOLDS Greg's clothes with care and lays them neatly into
the boat, as instructed. There's less jibber-jabber now. I suppose she
is tired—like all of us. I'm working on adrenaline, so I didn't notice
the time until darkness fell. This feels safer in the moonlight. We've
been at it two hours now, even with three of us digging.

I push the boat from the water's edge one last time, this time from
the path side. We watch it drift off downstream in the moonlight.

'Goodbye, Greg,' Lyssa murmurs.

'No time for sentimentality now,' I mumble.

'I dunno why you are looking out to the water. He's over there, in
the field,' Preston says, pointing.

We clean the spade in the river and place it back in Greg's car.
Then we drive our separate ways back home to the flats. We had all
ended up at different parking spots, forking off from the central
meeting place.

*I still have work on the agenda. I make a mental list on my drive
home.*

Skip number ten at the dump by Strawberry Corner is my first
stop tomorrow morning, to dump Lyssa's knife set—minus the one

Alyssa sent to Robyn, the one left with Greg's body, and the one resting on my driver's seat in a plastic bag coated with Greg Holstead's blood.

I deposit my car in the car park at the flats, pick up my rucksack and head out for a walk. As suggested by Lyssa, I take the convoluted way, crossing the road and using the underpass back under the road to find Louise's green car. I open the car door, as instructed, and hide the knife under the seat, jamming so far in that it does not shift. I tick off the mental to-do list of my insurance plan:

Clothes—tick.

Body—tick.

Boat—tick.

Knife—tick.

Knife set—tomorrow morning.

SIXTY-EIGHT

LYSSA

I OPEN my newsfeed to see the local news site.

LOCAL SOLICITOR MISSING

Police report that local man Greg Holstead, 55, is suspected missing in the River Tyne near Haddington.

He was reported missing by his fiancé, Louise Lacey, on Thursday. She led police to where she had found his car, parked by Haddington Coronation Trees. The car park is owned by Lamp of Lothian Trust. A boat, believed to belong to Mr. Holstead, was found abandoned at the weir in Haddington on Wednesday and was reported on the East Lothian Courier *Facebook page. Police tell us Ms Lacey identified clothes found in the boat as belonging to Mr. Holstead. Police divers are being deployed at the scene.*

Witnesses are being sought for any sightings of Mr. Holstead (pictured with his fiancé below) between 7pm Tuesday and 1pm Thursday. He is last known to have texted he was heading out on

business at 7pm on Tuesday evening. Anyone with any
information in this regard is asked to contact Police.

I have little time to digest this news. I breathe in, smoothing down my black dress. I pop on a pink lip to brighten up my face, and then wipe it off. I'm not in a bright mood. I don't want another solicitor fancying me.

My appointment is in ten minutes—and on this same street. How many solicitors does one town need? And why were we ever friends with that one? I feel every step I make these days. It's like my movements are narrated by another voice, the one in my head, as if I'm observing myself. Once in the building, I take a seat and wait in silence until my name is called.

'What can we do for you today? Your husband's will, I believe?' The lady solicitor asks.

'It's complicated. My husbands will left me nothing. However, I have found this will in boxes saying otherwise. Sorry if it's a bit crushed.' I flatten it out on the desk, and she moves it towards her.

'Your executor, the one dealing with the will, you should—' I cut her off.

'Greg Holstead.'

'Oh.'

'You'll have heard the news.'

'Yes.'

'This is my husband's copy of his will, which was missing. The one that Mr. Holstead, my solicitor and executor, has doesn't match this one. This one here leaves almost everything to me. Mr. Holstead's 's version left it all to another woman abroad, claiming to be Duncan's wife. She benefits also in this one, but in a smaller fashion.' It's funny that I'm now able to sum this up in such a short paragraph. My life edit.

She raises an eyebrow.

'Leave it with me. I'll do some digging to see if we can work out what has gone on here. If this is the most up-to-date will, you'll be able to contest the other one.'

'You don't understand. I don't think this will is more up-to-date. I think the will Mr. Holstead was working with was fake.'

'If that is the case, this is very serious.' She fumbles for the words. 'But how could this come about?'

'I suspect Mr. Holstead was involved in an illegal matter.'

'What? Fraud? This is quite a scenario you are painting. It will take quite some time to sort out, especially ... given the circumstances of Mr. Holstead's ... erm ... disappearance.'

'I can wait.'

'You fully believe you're the victim of fraud?'

'Yes. I am the victim.'

SIXTY-NINE

RHIANNON

Four months later

'HAVE YOU SEEN?' Preston murmurs. With no customary screeching, and given the colour of his complexion, I deduce something is amiss.

'What?'

'The body has been found.'

I feel cold, and then warm, and finally queasy. I release my masseter muscle and suck in a deep breath, holding onto the wall.

'Okay, we planned for this eventuality. Keep calm.'

'Right, Rhiannon, the same calm you were when the police came a-knocking the day after the event and you shit yourself. When it turned out your tap-and-go at the petrol station just hadn't gone through?'

I can't bring myself to laugh, although it had been a source of amusement later that day.

'Where did you see it?' I ask.

'*East Lothian Courier* page.'

'Okay, what do they know?'

'Here we go. I'll read it.'

BODY FOUND IN HADDINGTON FIELD

A body has been found in an East Lothian field, with emergency services rushing to the scene on Sunday evening.

A horrified farmer, while harvesting his crops, discovered the remains buried at the side of his field. Police have since confirmed that a 55-year-old man was pronounced dead at the scene. Police are treating the death as suspicious.

A Police Scotland spokesperson said: 'Around 10.45am on Sunday 20 August, we received a report of a body in a farmer's field adjacent to the River Tyne in Haddington. A 55-year-old man was pronounced dead at the scene. Enquiries are ongoing, but there appears to be suspicious circumstances, and foul play is evident. A report will be submitted to the Procurator Fiscal.'

Rumours are circulating that the death may be related to the disappearance of local solicitor Gregory Holstead four months ago. He was believed to have committed suicide in the river at the time, but his body was never recovered.

Anyone with any information is advised to contact Crimestoppers.

We both flinch at a bang at the door. Preston runs to his room, poking his head out

'Oh, fuck! The rozzers are here,' he whispers.

'So quick? Why, though?' I whisper back.

'I don't know!'

Two more urgent thumps on the door divert my attention away from him. I inhale, exhale, and then open the door to view Alyssa carrying two bottles of her favourite sweet wine.

'Sorry for booting the door. My hands were full. Celebration time! My insurance policy money has come in.' She scans our faces, and her expression falls. 'What's wrong?'

'It is happening.'

'Oh God!'

'And now, the time has come when we hope *our* insurance policy falls into place,' I mutter, as I close the door behind her.

SEVENTY

RHIANNON

One month later

I SHOW the police through to the living room and perch on the sofa. I recognise the policewoman, the same one who told me about Duncan dying more than a year ago. I'm still wearing my new Karen Millen jacket, having just minutes ago returned from my rounds. I had walked my daily circuit via Eskside to check Louise hadn't cleared her car out since 'the event.' Over the past few months, her resident brown cardigan and newspapers had only been added to with another jacket, a plastic cup, and some random detritus. Today, however, was different. Today, her green car was being lifted onto a truck with a police car in attendance.

As I wandered back, I'd noticed that Greg's office sported a new 'to let' sign. He didn't even own *that* building.

'Can you tell me about your relationship with Mr. Holstead?' The woman begins.

'Yes, as you know, he was a family friend and our solicitor. I was devastated over my husband's death, and I'm afraid he took advantage of me at my most vulnerable. I wouldn't have normally associated with him on a personal level. We went on a few dates.'

'Would you describe yourself as his girlfriend?'

'No. It was a casual thing. You must understand: I was in an emotional state with the death of my husband.'

'Emotional?' She looks at me with narrowed eyes.

I indicate our wedding photo sitting on the sideboard and reframe, 'Grief. Not emotional as in hysterical. It was, and still is, a heavy weight. Especially in the circumstances, which turned out to be a misunderstanding, and then a fraud ...' I fix her with a stare, and she lowers her head. 'It was ... difficult to process. Our fling was a distraction from that. Greg was so keen on me, and I suppose it helped my confidence. It was a comfort.'

'You knew about his relationship with Ms. Lacey?'

'Now, here's the thing—I didn't know she was his fiancé. He described her as a crazy stalker.'

'Men often do,' she says, too quickly. She zips her lip again.

But I nod, perceiving an opening. 'Yes, that is what I put it down to. Men who claim crazy exes are often a red flag, aren't they?'

She gives a tight-lipped smile.

'But then, she did behave threateningly, too.'

The policewoman leans forward. 'Did she?'

'Wrote me a letter. At least I guessed it was from her. It was a poison pen letter, you know, an old-fashioned one with the letters cut out from the paper.'

'Do you have it?'

'Oh no. I binned it. I didn't want a fuss. I knew she was a silly, jealous woman. I rose above it. I'm not the insecure type, you understand. Greg had other women he'd see.' I tick them off on my fingers. 'Erm ... Karina, and what's her name ... Robyn. He told me about them.' I cross my legs, remove my jacket, and relax against the John Lewis cushions.

She scribbles in her pad. 'And you weren't concerned about that?'

'No, no. It was an open relationship, if you could call it a relationship at all.'

She checks her notebook again. 'And he split with you to return to his ... um ... fiancé?'

'No. It was other way around. I ended the liaison. He was distraught. He actually suggested we marry at one point, but for me, it was too soon. Something did not add up with him, you know. Later, when I found the will—you'll know all about that case, of course—where it turned out I *was* the first wife and main beneficiary.'

'Yes.' Her head drops.

'I couldn't believe it, but at the same time, suddenly everything made sense. He was besotted with me in the end, though. When we believed he'd committed suicide, I wasn't sure if was guilt or a broken heart that tipped him over the edge.'

I hang up my jacket as the police leave. I will be staying in this flat for some time yet while the will is contested. I pop my Michael Kors bag down to fetch a hammer from the tool kit. I'm keeping the tools now, too. A lady never knows when she might need a tool kit.

I pick up the crucifix, which lies propped against the wall the police walked by a minute ago. Jesus Christ can't be left sitting against a skirting board—that would be uncouth. It's best hung up. After all, no one would ever think to look for a murder weapon that's in full view.

The End

EPILOGUE
LYSSA

One year later...

PRESTON HAULS off the red velvet cover with great aplomb, revealing the painting of Winifred Orr against the wall of The Grand House.

A cheer goes up, which sends my doggos into a frenzy.

Sidney stands rubbing his chin with one hand. 'Is that crucifix in the painting the same as the one in the hall, Lyssa?'

'It looks like,' Debbie comments, squinting close-up.

'Ooh. So, it does, but no. I bought my cross in a flea market in the Canaries,' I explain with a flip of my hand.

The small gathering disperses back to several easy chairs in the living area, muttering about holidays to Tenerife and the like.

'And in today's news, dare we mention it ... the guilty verdict!'

'Preston, you can't!' Sidney scolds.

'Oh, yes I can, and I do.' He looks delighted.

'I didn't think Louise would be capable of murder,' Debbie chips in.

'Open and shut case. What about her putting a tracker on his car?' Preston begins. 'No wonder she took the police right to where it was parked when he went missing.'

Jan interrupts, 'We all knew he wasn't up to your standard, Lyssa.'

I smile. *Good old Jan.* I pass her some canapés.

'It says here ...' Preston begins

'Preston you're not on your phone, are you?' Sidney admonishes him with a playful smack on the hand.

'I want to get the details right. It says they had some sort of scam going on. He'd romance these women in this flat they ran as an AirBnB up Leith. He'd pretend it was his place, to hide their set-up. Then he'd con them.'

Tony blushes and butts in, 'I kinda knew about him and Louise being together. It was Louise's money that paid for that flat in Leith, although they owned it in joint names. It was part of his training to use women with money. He said it was to even up the imbalance of women using men ...'

I throw Tony a look, and he trails off. 'Excuse me,' he mumbles and leaves the room. Rhiannon follows.

'I knew he stayed at Louise's a lot,' Debbie adds. 'My auntie said he was always coming and going, banging the front door when she was trying to sleep. I never thought much about it until later.'

I glare at her and she shrugs. *You might have mentioned this, Debbie,* I think. I'm still holding court, however.

'He must have thought he'd hit the jackpot with me and this house—before he fell in love with me, I mean. He'd swindled Karina Summerfield out of her car. And he was in the process off conning Robyn Khafoor out of her substantial divorce settlement. Louise would get jealous, though, and let her emotions run away with her at times. He'd try to use that to his benefit to make the women paranoid. I couldn't have cared less, so it didn't work with me.' I laugh and wave a hand. 'I was suspicious of him from the beginning, you know, a gut feeling. By the end, I was only going with him to find out more about

Duncan's death and the will. It never added up to me. At one point, I even checked his phone!'

'You never!' Debbie exclaims.

'I did!' I laugh. I must have thought I was a spy. He thought he was clever, though. Got Louise to pretend to be Kwai Tan at one point in his messages. He nearly had me going there. But all he had done was changed Louise's name in his contacts. He suggested I'd done the same with Jill's name on my phone. He suggested she was another man in disguise. He was so jealous and possessive. '

'Bet that Louise thought she'd got away with the fake suicide thing, too,' Jan adds between mouthfuls. 'It was pretty well-planned. He wasn't found for months. I read about it earlier.' She pulls a face. 'She was a bit lax, though, leaving her knives here and there, the daft beggar.'

I laugh. 'I know! You couldn't make it up. I'd have done a better job myself. Excuse me.' I leave to powder my nose. In the hallway, I hang back, aware of Tony and Rhiannon sitting on the stairs. I hover to eavesdrop.

'I've always struggled with his work, but he seemed so successful. All the other guys admired him. I was rubbish at life, and when he told me I needed a new mindset, I believed he was helping me. I'm sorry I was ever involved with him. I guess I was almost ... brainwashed.'

'It's a lesson, I guess,' Rhiannon says.

'I think I'll forgive him—for my own good. People are flawed, aren't they, Rhiannon?'

'Indeed, they are,' she replies.

THE TRUE STORY OF THE PAINTING

The real Henrietta and more

Around 1967, George Cunningham decided to renovate an old outbuilding behind the baker's shop he owned. The baker's shop was known as Dickson's Bakers and stood at 68/70 High Street, Musselburgh. The outbuilding was previously a 'but and ben' property, and then a henhouse accessed via a close at the side of the baker's shop. He made plans to make a room for his children to play billiards and asked his father (George Senior) to do the renovations for him. During the renovation, George Senior discovered a false ceiling and rafters that had been cut away to conceal an old oil painting wrapped in naval flags. One of the shop assistants passed the painting onto her son, who worked for Historic Scotland. They called the painting *The Pinkie Painting* at this time.

All went quiet for years, and they forgot all about the painting. In the early to mid 1970s, George's niece Isabel was watching a BBC TV programme about restoring paintings. They happened to air someone from Historic Scotland, who used the painting as an example.

In the early 1980s, George's daughter-in-law Lynn visited Historic Scotland to view the restored painting and confirmed that the painting belonged to the Cunningham family.

Again, it was forgotten about, until George passed away in 2004. His wife, Evelyn, went to view the painting at The Historic Scotland Conservation Centre in 2005 and was allowed to take the painting away. She was told that although it was of historical interest, it had no monetary value. Henrietta, as the woman in the painting was nicknamed (after the henhouse) sits above a door in a modest terraced villa in Inveresk Road, Musselburgh, to this day.

Thanks to Morag Barclay (George's daughter) and Evelyn, for the whole story and the tea and cakes.

Who was she?

There is some speculation the subject could be Mary Oswald, a generous widowed woman from Inveresk Village, who did indeed feed and clothe the poor from a soup kitchen at Musselburgh town hall. The old town hall in Musselburgh stands directly opposite the site of Dickson's Bakers (now Baynes).

The tunnels under Musselburgh also exist. I have accounts of tunnels from the river heading up to an Inveresk house and coming out into their ballroom fireplace. The story about Mary Queen of Scots losing her ring there is still spoken of.

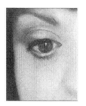

ABOUT THE AUTHOR

Emelle Adams lives in East Lothian, Scotland, with her son and a white cat.

https://www.facebook.com/EmelleAdamsauthor

ALSO BY EMELLE ADAMS

The Nursing Her Wrath series follows the vengeful thoughts and actions of a series of Scottish women brought up together in the same small Scottish town. These dark, sometimes comedic, fast-paced psychological tales keep you guessing until the very end.

The Bucket List

Angela is running out of time. Already 48 and terminally ill with brain cancer she starts a bucket list '50 things to do before 50'. But what she really wants to do before she kicks the bucket isn't 'walking with alpacas' or being an extra in a film or even finishing her memoirs. It is seeking revenge on all those who wronged her over the years, all those who definitely deserve to die before she does, all those who would otherwise get to see how the story ends when Angela certainly won't, or will she?

The Revenge Pawn

Following a failed marriage, Rhiannon returns to the parochial Scottish town she grew up in and immediately falls foul of childhood 'queen bee' Kimberly.

Beautiful, successful, and married, Kim has everything—including dark secrets—but she is still a bully who uses people like pawns. In the game they're playing, Rhiannon has nothing left to lose ... until she finds a series of family letters and realises that revenge is in the blood and a true queen can move in any direction at all ...

Printed in Great Britain
by Amazon

36228513R00175